There had been a lot of changes in the past thirty years, and Julian West was full of questions about life in the year 2000 . . . but he was not prepared for the answers. . . .

"When I die—"

"Die?" the doctor almost shouted. "Julian! You're not contemplating suicide? I know you're unhappy about some of the changes that have taken place and the difficulties you're having acclimating yourself. But suicide isn't the answer."

"Oh, no, you don't understand. I meant eventually, through natural causes. When I'm older."

The doctor shook his head. "You know, during the past few weeks you've asked a hundred questions, and by the time we've answered them, we wind up saying *we don't have that any more*. Things like money, banks, cities, pollution, population explosion . . ."

"What's that got to do with my realizing that death—"

"Jule, *we don't die any more*."

EQUALITY:
IN THE YEAR 2000

by
MACK REYNOLDS

ace books
A Division of Charter Communications Inc.
A GROSSET & DUNLAP COMPANY
1120 Avenue of the Americas
New York, New York 10036

Other Ace Books by Mack Reynolds:

ABILITY QUOTIENT

DAY AFTER TOMORROW

DEPRESSION OR BUST

DAWNMAN PLANET

FIVE WAY SECRET AGENT

MERCENARY FROM TOMORROW

GALACTIC MEDAL OF HONOR

PLANETARY AGENT X

THE RIVAL RIGELIANS

POLICE PATROL: 2000 A.D.

SATELLITE CITY

To Arthur C. Clarke

With whom I couldn't agree more when he wrote in his excellent PROFILES OF THE FUTURE: *It is impossible to predict the future, and all attempts to do so in any detail appear ludicrous within a very few years. . . . If this book seems completely reasonable and all my extrapolations convincing, I will not have succeeded in looking very far ahead; for the one fact about the future of which we can be certain is that it will be utterly fantastic.*

INTRODUCTION

Almost a century ago, an obscure, unsuccessful writer named Edward Bellamy wrote a novel, *Looking Backward*, the success of which was as much a surprise to him as it was to the rest of the world. Indeed, it shortly became the most influential Utopian book ever written. Sales were in the millions; it was translated into twenty languages; countless editions were issued and it has never gone out of print. It deeply influenced such men as John Dewey, William Allen White, Norman Thomas, Thorstein Veblen. Franklin D. Roosevelt reported that in his youth, it was his "Bible." Not too long ago, when a committee of three literary personalities—John Dewey, Charles Beard, and Edward Weeks—was named to designate the twenty-five most influential books published since 1885, Bellamy's novel was voted unanimously as second only to Marx' *Das Kapital*.

But a century is a long time, and although *Looking Backward* is still highly readable, even inspiring to those who envision a better world, it is very dated. Much of what Bellamy foresaw in portraying his future society has already been accomplished; much can never be.

So it was that I had decided to use the fundamental plot, the basic characters, and aim for the same goal as did Bellamy—a portrayal of the world in 2000 A.D. as it might be, if man comes to his senses. The novel, dedicated to Edward Bellamy, was entitled *Looking Backward: From the Year 2000*.

As mentioned, Bellamy was amazed at the reception of his Utopian story. All over the country, "Bellamy Clubs" sprang up, particularly in the colleges. Thousands of letters poured in, praising, criticizing, questioning, sometimes reviling various aspects. In defense, he wrote a sequel, expanding his ideas, going into more detail. It was entitled *Equality*, was unsuccessful, and soon disappeared from the scene.

The present writer finds himself in the same predicament. Letters began pouring in—not all of them flattering. In defense, I have written my own sequel, *Equality: In the Year 2000*.

Though a sequel to *Looking Backward: From the Year 2000*, this novel can be read without a knowledge of the first book. However, it will do no harm to have a brief summary of what has gone before.

When Julian West, playboy multimillionaire, is informed by his doctor that his heart gives him at most two years to live, he seeks out the top authority on stasis—placing bodies into artificial hibernation. With the hope that science will evolve to the point where his disease is curable and he can be revived, he creates a foundation to finance the radical experiment.

Julian had expected it to be a matter of a few years at most. He is flabbergasted to be awakened thirty-three years later in the apartment of Academician Raymond Leete, his wife Martha, and daughter Edith. They have been given the task of helping him adjust to the geometrically developing changes.

Leete points out that since 1940, when Julian was a child, human knowledge has been doubling every eight years, so that now the race has 256 times the knowledge that prevailed then. The computers and automation are in full swing, so that only two percent of the population are needed to produce all that the country can consume and ninety-eight percent are on Guaranteed Annual Income. There have been radical changes in government, in industry, in the arts and sciences. Julian finds himself at sea in almost every field. Money is no longer in use, so all his efforts to perpetuate his fortune were meaningless. Cities no longer exist, nor wars, nor pollution, nor the threat of the exhaustion of the planet's resources—none of the problems of his own time. There is no crime, no juvenile delinquents or the use of drugs.

He cannot believe so many changes could take place in but a third of a century. Leete asks him to consider, in comparison, the changes that took place between June 1914 . . . June 1947, the same length of time.

The book ends with Julian disillusioned with this world as a Utopia—at least for him. Interlingua, an international language, has been established and the new generations do not even speak English. The Leetes had been especially trained to take care of him, as an interesting experiment. But the generation gap is such now, with human knowledge over 250 times greater than in his youth, that Julian cannot even communicate with the average person. When he proposes to Edith, she points out the impossibility. And he is too far behind, at the age of thirty-five, to ever catch up. By the time he got through the equivalent of grammar school, human knowledge would have doubled again.

He says, in despair, "I've been calling this Utopia, but it isn't. For me, it's dystopia, the exact opposite. I'm a freak. Why did you ever awaken me?"

Edith shook her head sadly. "It wasn't my decision to make, Julian. I was against it."

"We are free today substantially; but the day will come when our Republic will be an impossibility. It will be an impossibility because wealth will become concentrated in the hands of a few. A Republic cannot exist upon bayonets; and when that day comes, when the wealth of the nation is in the hands of a few, then we must rely upon the wisdom of the best elements of the country to readjust the laws of the nation to the changed conditions."

James Madison, 4th President of the U.S.
Father of the Constitution

Chapter One

The Year 2 New Calendar

Old people's skills, experience, and knowledge seldom make them authorities, and are no longer critical factors in our culture. The speed and pervasiveness of social change now transforms the world within a generation, so that the experience of the old becomes largely irrelevant to the young.

— Irving Roscow, *Social Scientist*

WHEN EDITH LEETE entered the sanctum of the Leete apartment in the high-rise building in the Julian West University City that morning, Julian was sitting at the desk before the auto-teacher. The expression on his face was one of sour despair.

1

He was a man in his mid-thirties. Youthfully fresh of complexion, handsome in the British aristocrat tradition, hair dark and thick, touches of premature gray at the temples and a small amount in his mustache, flat of stomach, square of shoulders, medium tall. There was a certain vulnerable quality about his eyes and mouth which women had always found attractive, though he had never known that.

She said, "*Bon maten, Jule.*"

"*Bon maten,*" he muttered, not quite graciously.

"How goes the study of Interlingua?" she asked in English.

"*Jupli mi legas gin. Des malpli mi komrenas gin.*"

"*Pri kio vi paroles?* What are you saying? The more you study it the less you understand it?"

"I wish to hell you people had stuck to English, instead of dreaming up this new international language."

She sank down in a seat and let her hands flop limply over the chair arms. "Nonsense, Jule. Interlingua is a scientific language. It works. Take spelling and pronunciation. They are absolutely phonetic and there are only five vowel sounds, where most of the old languages have twenty or more. Each letter has one sound only, and a sound is always indicated by the same letter. English was a bastard language—goodness knows how anyone ever learned it, including me. Take the word *can*. It means a container; it can also be a verb meaning to *can* something in a container; it also means you *can*, or are able to, do something; and it also means, spelled *C-a-n-n-e-s*, a town in southern France. In American idiom it could mean to dismiss or fire someone, and in British idiom it meant a tankard.

"Or take this sentence: 'There are three ways of spelling *to*.' Now how would you go about spelling that, *t-o*, *t-o-o*, or *t-w-o*?"

Julian had to laugh. "I admit we had some lulus."

Edith continued, "And take grammar and syntax. Interlingua is so ingeniously devised that in place of the usual maze of rules occupying a sizable volume on grammar, we have only sixteen short rules, which may be written comfortably on a single sheet of notepaper."

"The vocabulary is so damned extensive. . . ."

"That's due to the many new words that have come into the language, but in actuality the rules are such that we cover several times the wordage you do in a given area. For example, we carry the principle of affixes through to its logical conclusion. In English you often form the feminine of a noun by adding e-s-s: author-authoress, lion-lioness. Often, but by no means always. You are not allowed to say bull-bulless or hero-heroess. In Interlingua, the feminine ending may be added to any noun, and so throughout the language there is no exception to any rule and no limit to its applicability."

"As you say, as you say . . ." Julian sighed. "At any rate, I'm plodding away. At this late date in life, it's a little difficult to get back into studying."

She frowned at his notepad and stylo. "What in the world are you doing?"

"Taking notes as I go along. I've always been a great note-taker when I study."

"So am I, but the days when Abe Lincoln made his notes on a wooden shovel with a piece of charcoal have passed."

He looked at her, not failing to note all over again

3

the blue eyes, the classical nose, the well-formed mouth, the golden hair cut boy-fashion. It was a healthy face, bright and open—projecting honesty, sincerity. She had told him that she had never worn any sort of cosmetic; it hadn't hurt her complexion any. He refused to let his eyes drop to her figure. He had long since been brought to the belief that her body was the most sexually attractive that he had ever seen, and he didn't wish to tantalize himself further. When he had mentioned marriage, she had pointed out, without cruelty, how impossible a permanent relationship between them would be: she, and her father and mother, had been selected to deal with this man from a third of a century past; to be brutally frank, they had learned to speak in what amounted to baby talk in order to communicate with him.

Now he asked, "What do you mean? This stylo isn't exactly a piece of charcoal. So far as I understand, it's sort of a combination pencil and pen, except you don't use either lead or ink, and it evidently lasts forever."

"The equivalent of lead or ink is in the *paper*," Edith explained patiently. "The advantage with this type of paper is that if you've mislaid your stylo, you can still write with anything pointed—even with a finger nail, if necessary. But what I meant was that your method of taking notes is antiquated."

He kept his eyes on her, wearily waiting for more. An hour didn't go by in the company of any of the Leetes but that they came up with something that floored him.

She said, "There, next to you, is the voco-typer. I

thought father explained it to you."

"Briefly. You talk into it and it types up what you say."

"There's more to it. I'm continually surprised, Jule, at your lack of knowledge of what was developing back in the 1960s and '70s, right under your nose. Most of what we have now in technological developments go back to your era, though I acknowledge it takes time—less so now than before—to bring a new breakthrough into widespread use. For instance, the basic facts of nuclear fission were known at least a decade before Einstein wrote President Roosevelt that an atomic bomb was possible."

"What in the dickens has this to do with my taking notes with my stylo?" Julian asked.

"I was leading up to the fact that even in your day, the voco-typer, the computer data banks, and the computer translators were already in embryo."

"Go on."

She indicated the voco-typer that sat to one side of him on the desk. "They've all been amalgamated. You speak your notes into the voco-typer. It is connected to the data banks; your notes are recorded and you can check back on them any time you wish. And, if you desired, you could record your notes in English now, and, after your Interlingua becomes more fluent, have your notes played back to you in that language—or any other language, for that matter."

"You mean that anyone at all can put anything he wants into the International Data Banks?"

"Of course. No problem. You see, all you could possibly write in your whole lifetime can be recorded on a disk no larger than your little fingernail, and about as thick."

"Well, how long do they keep the record?"

"Forever. Fifty years from now, you might have some reason to check back on some of the notes you take today. They'll be on file. Then there are other aspects. Suppose, a century or two from now, some biographer wishes to check back on your notes in order to do your life. There they are. Can you imagine how some historian in your time would have loved to have the notes of, say, Thomas Jefferson—made while he was composing the Declaration of Independence? I suggest that you have Information send you its material on filing and cross references. Speeds things up so that you'll be able to check back more easily."

Julian said indignantly, "Just one minute. Suppose there's something in my notes I don't want some goddamned biographer to see?"

"Don't be silly. Anything of yours in the data banks can be wiped any time you wish. Your notes don't have to remain if you don't want them there. Or you can simply make a requirement that they are available to no one but you until such and such a date—or never."

"Suppose I'm out somewhere without a voco-typer handy?"

"Then simply record your material by voice into your transceiver, ordering that it be put into the data banks in print."

He shook his head. "Every day, I realize all over again how much there is for me to learn. Why, it'll take me the better part of my life to reach the point you're at now. How about a drink, Edie?"

"I'll get it," she offered, rising. She headed to the auto-bar. "Scotch for you, I suppose?"

There was a distressed look in her eyes when she handed him his whisky. "I don't know what to say, Jule. I heard father tell you about the so-called knowledge explosion the other day, but I wonder if you completely followed through on the ramifications."

"You mean that quote from Dr. Robert Oppenheimer that human knowledge is doubling every eight years?"

She nodded. "You see, he made that statement about 1955. So let's take the year 1940 as the takeoff point. In the following eight years, various major breakthroughs were made, including nuclear fission, the first space ship, the German V-2, the first practical radar, and, in medicine, penicillin and the sulfas. Between 1948 and 1956 came additional breakthroughs: the conquest of polio, the modern computer, the first Sputnik in space, transistors. By this time, doubling each eight years, human knowledge was four times what it had been in 1940. Between 1956 and 1964, organ transplants; man went into space, following his history-long companion, the dog. Lasers and masers made their appearance, the supersonic aircraft, and nuclear fision, and human knowledge was eight times what it was in 1940. By 1972 it was sixteen times, we were on the moon, constructing space platforms, and relaying communications from scores of artificial satellites. Among other achievements, for the first time a living man—you—was put into artificial hibernation, to be awakened thirty-three years in the future.''

She took a sip of her wine and regarded him thoughtfully. ''And while you slept, the knowledge explosion went on. In 1980 knowledge was thirty-two times that of 1940; by 1988 it was sixty-four; by 1996 it was one-hundred twenty-eight times greater than in 1940. And shortly, in 2004, or the year 4 New Calendar, the multiple will be two-hundred fifty-six.''

Julian shook his head wearily.

Edith continued, ''Suppose we put it another way. Let us say a child was born in the year 1940 and that, given modern medicine, he lives to be ninety-six years of age, dying in an accident. That would mean in the year 2036, using the old calendar. By that time, Jule, human knowledge will be 4096 times as much as when he was born. Believe me, it even shakes us up. Way back in your day, a Julius Horwitz of the New York Department of Welfare, put it bluntly. 'The aged in a big city have no economic status; they have no status in the household, they have no vocational skills to pass on to the younger generation. Their special problem is survival in a society which finds their minds and bodies superfluous.'

''Well, we cherish our older people these days, as we do our children; nevertheless, the generation gap is present with a vengeance. In fact, the gap begins no more than halfway through a generation: the thirteen-year-olds show impatience with the twenty-five-year-olds.''

''What are you leading up to, Edie?'' he asked.

She eyed him compassionately. ''Jule, when you went into stasis, human knowledge was sixteen times what it had been in 1940. Do you remember 1940?"

"Vaguely; I was a young child."

"When you went into stasis, to what degree were you up on the latest scientific and technological breakthroughs?"

He snorted in self-depreciation. "I had already been left far behind. Half the time I couldn't even follow the science, medical, and space articles in *Time* and *Newsweek*, though they were written for the layman. I never did figure out what lasers were, and the workings of computers simply floored me; I recall reading about one fellow programming a computer to play chess and it beat a chess buff. Space travel was all very interesting to watch on TV but when I tried to read a bit about it, I was at sea instead of in space. The simplest articles on the subject were too technical for me. The data banks, which were just beginning to start up in earnest . . . I read of a new storage device which would allow for every book in the Library of Congress to be stored in an area a couple of square feet in size. Things like that simply boggled my mind. I gave up trying to keep up. But what's the point, Edie?"

"Your studying, Jule. Oh, I admire your spirit— trying to catch up, at least to the point where you can conduct your daily life rationally in this world of the twenty-first century, as it would have been called under the old calendar. Most important, of course, is learning Interlingua, and there is no reason you can't do that. But the magnitude of the rest of your problem is appalling."

It was unreasonable, he knew, but nevertheless he was irritated. "Why? I'm only a bit more than a generation behind you. There is no difference between my brain and yours. I'm not stupid. I can take the same classes your young people take. I can catch up."

She sighed. "Jule—Jule. . . . You are going to have to start from absolute scratch. The education you had, a bachelor's degree, is now meaningless. By the time you are through the equivalent of what you used to call grammar school, human knowledge will have doubled again. It will be 512 times what it was when you were a child in 1940."

"I don't want or expect to develop into a nuclear scientist. If the kids can pick up an ordinary layman's education, I can too," he said stubbornly. "We've been over this before."

She shook her head in despair. "Even that, Jule. Today's children take chemical and electronic stimulants—temporarily, while they are studying—to increase their intelligence quotients and receptivity."

"Well, why can't I take them too?"

"Because you are in your middle thirties. Actually, of course, you are pushing seventy, but physically and mentally you are a man in his thirties. You see, Jule, a person continues to grow, both mentally and physically, until he is approximately twenty-five years of age. From then on, he begins to deteriorate. We can slow down the process, but we cannot eliminate it entirely. The stimulants we utilize to increase intelligence and learning aptitude work best on youth. After the age of twenty-five, they slack off in effectiveness. Indeed, at the age of fifty or so, they are meaningless. Perhaps this will be overcome in the future, as new advances are made in the field, but for the present the use of such stimulants would not do you very much good.''

''Jesus!'' Julian protested. ''So even the eight-year-olds have a head start on me.''

''In more ways than one,'' she agreed unhappily. ''This is their world: they were born into it; they are perfectly at home in it. For you, it is as though you had landed on an alien planet. Everything is new to you; they have been assimilating their surroundings ever since they were in the cradle.''

He gazed at her for one more frustrated moment, then turned back to the auto-teacher and flicked it on. ''Nevertheless,'' he muttered, ''I'll stick to it at least to the point where I can order a hamburger in a restaurant.''

She frowned at his back, even as she finished her drink. ''What is a hamburger?''

''I'll never tell,'' he smirked at her over his shoulder. ''That's one thing I know about that you don't.'' But then he relented. ''People used to eat them, for some reason or other not quite clear to me now that I'm acquainted with present-day cuisine.''

Edith stood and went over to toss her glass into the auto-bar's disposal chute.

''Well, I'll leave you to your studies and go to my room to do my own.''

He blinked at her. ''Your own? I thought you were out of school.''

She had to laugh, albeit somewhat ruefully. ''Just to keep up with developments, I spend two hours a day at concentrated study, Jule. So does everybody else who doesn't wish to fall by the wayside with

what's happening in the world. I'll see you at breakfast with Mother and Father."

He looked at her blankly. "Do they continue to
study too?"

"Father puts in four hours a day, seven days a
week. Of course, he is still doing medical research,
and attempts to keep up with the latest."

Chapter Two

The Year 1956

UNLIKE SOME, Julian West seldom realized that he
was dreaming while it was going on. The past usually
came to him with such vivid accuracy that he thought
he was actually experiencing it. To call most of them
dreams was stretching a point. They were more accurately nightmares. Even under a sedative, he was
unable to avoid them.

Now he was reliving an experience he'd had some
years before going into stasis. It was on a trip to
Tangier, Morocco, that fabulous city nestled on the
Straits of Hercules and forming the link between
Africa and Egypt, back when it was still an Interna-
tional Zone governed by eight European countries.

He landed at the Tangier airport. As usual, the
administration building and its environs were swarm-

ing, mostly with men and boys. Save for a dozen or so ladies in European dress, obviously awaiting passengers on arriving flights, the handful of women were wearing the shapeless, tentlike white cotton hail which came over the head and, in combination with a veil, shielded the face completely except for the eyes, then dropped all the way to the ground so that not even the feet could be seen. The costume of the men was more diverse. Turbans of a half-dozen varieties could be observed. Some had on the fez, that rimless, red-colored hat. Still others wore wool knit hats, in such condition it seemed a self-respecting rat wouldn't have slept in them. Almost universally, the men were garbed in the djellaba, handwoven of wool or camel hair. It was a useful garment, Julian knew, warm at night as a blanket, protection from the sun during the day, and it repelled rain. In fact, there was a hood that could be pulled up over the head in bad weather.

The airplane from Gibralter was a small craft, seating but twenty-one. When Julian disembarked, he and the other travelers were immediately surrounded by a small crowd of peddlers, hotel solicitors, money changers, and pimps. An old hand, Julian snarled at them in French, and was able to make his way toward the immigration and customs office inside. He could change money in town, at one of the many booths on Pasteur Boulevard; he'd get a better rate than from any of the touts here. Actually, all currencies were legal tender in the International Zone, but the most widely accepted was French francs and you often got better prices using them.

Customs and immigration were the merest of formalities. The immigration man stamped his passport without checking if the photo inside corresponded with Julian's face.

Two barefooted teenagers, thin and grimy, had scurried up to take his two heavy leather bags as soon as they had been checked. He could have carried the luggage himself. But he didn't want to go through the hassle of telling them so, and simply followed the urchins out to the parking lot where he located a Chico Cab. They were, he had decided, the smallest taxis in the world: little Fiat 500s from Italy.

He put the bags on the seat next to the driver and climbed into the back.

"El Minzah Hotel," he said, after giving both of the boys a quarter. They yelled for more, but he ignored them. They would have protested had he given them a dollar—or five dollars, for that matter.

The countryside into town was typical of North Africa from the Atlantic to the Nile: incredibly dusty, worn down, poverty stricken. It seemed impossible that any of the tiny farms could support the rag-clothed families who lived in the little one-room shacks made of tin cans, waste wood, cardboard from cartons. They passed a few scrawny dogs from time to time, some scrawnier chickens, an occasional burro, a couple of motheaten camels, and a multitude of filthy children.

The driver entered town from the southwest, speeding along the Avenue d'Espana, which paralleled the half-crescent bay around which the city of Tangier is built.

Julian liked the city. It was one of the most exotic in the world. Founded by the Phoenicians several millennia ago, a dozen nations had controlled it since. Its palace-crowned Kabash overlooked the Spanish coast across the way, and in the distance Gibraltar, that most impressive landfall on earth, reared its bulk. It still appeared today much as the Baghdad of Scheherazade's time must have looked, with its narrow winding streets which allowed for no vehicle, its teeming *souks* with their produce and handicrafts of all Morocco; filthy, swarming with flies, but overflowing with some of the most beautiful fruit and vegetables to be found, products of the oases to the south.

They were going through the Spanish section of Tangier now. Ahead and to the right, Julian could make out the Port de Peche, a dock and basin supposedly devoted to fishing, but the sleek-looking boats, he knew, were smugglers. Among them were former German E-Boats, French torpedo boats, British anti-submarine craft. Immediately after the Second World War they had become surplus and a drug on the market, using too much fuel to be converted into pleasure craft. Smuggling was legal in Tangier, and they broke no law running cigarettes and such over to Europe.

The boulevard had been circling the bay. Now the driver took a sharp left and started up a rather steep, narrow street, heading for the modern European section of the city. It looked more like the French Riviera, or a California town, not anything you'd expect to find in Morocco.

After a couple of blocks, which were becoming more modern in architecture by the moment, the taxi pulled up before the El Minzah Hotel. There was a huge black standing out front, garbed in what the hotel owners probably thought was the type of clothing once worn by the Sultan's bodyguard, complete to a golden sash with a vicious-looking scimitar thrust through it.

Two maroon-uniformed bellhops, wearing the fez, scurried forth for his bags. Julian paid the cabby with an American dollar, ignored his protests, and followed his luggage inside.

The El Minzah was the best hotel in Tangier, and he had reserved one of the twin penthouse suites. He invariably stayed here when in the International Zone; the view over the straits was superb. He went through the routine of registering, the fez-hatted manager, oily as ever, bobbing and gushing.

In the suite, Julian didn't tip the bellhops. In Morocco you didn't tip until you paid your bill, at which time you left a sizable percent of your tab with the desk clerk who supposedly spread it around to everyone who had served you. Julian suspected that most of it went into the pockets of the manager and clerk.

At the moment, he didn't bother to unpack, or even to summon a valet to do it for him. He simply tossed his homburg on the bureau and started out again. He felt like a drink or two and then possibly a late lunch; it had been a long time since he had enjoyed a Moroccan *cous cous*.

The El Minzah was situated just below the Place de France, the center plaza of the European area, and about halfway to the Grand Zocco, the largest of the town's open souks located on the edge of the native section. Julian headed down in the direction of the zocco, mildly surprised at the number of people on the streets. He came to the Rue America du Sud and turned left. He was headed for Dean's, in his opinion one of the outstanding bars in the world, comparable to Sloppy Joe's in Havana, Sheppard's in Cairo, even Harry's in Venice, that old standby of Papa Hemingway's. Such oases, considered Julian, were saloons with souls.

Just as he was about to cross the street, a youngster sidled up to him. He was possibly ten years old, with a beautiful Arab face, light coffee of complexion, dazzling white teeth, and the wide, sad, dark brown eyes of a gazelle.

Julian was initially of the belief that the child was a beggar and reached for his pocket, though ordinarily he refrained.

However, the boy did not hold out his hand. "Fuckee, fuckee—suckee, suckee?"

Julian was horrified. He had been accosted before by both male and female child prostitutes in Tangier, a world-renowned watering place for homosexuals who preferred youth, but never by one so young as this. A wave of renewed contempt for Moslem mores and customs swept over him. He knew, for instance, that by Moslem law a girl could be given in marriage at the age of eight. In theory her husband was not to bed her until she had menstruated—but that was only the theory.

He shook his head at the boy and crossed the street to Dean's.

To his surprise, the only occupant of the bar, besides Dean and his two waiters, was an old friend from college days.

"Roy!"

"Jule, for Christ's sake!"

Roy London was seated at a small table near the door, obviously so that he could watch the passers-by. Now he rose to his feet and they shook hands enthusiastically.

Julian said, "I thought I had heard you were up in London working for Reuters." He turned: "A couple of those Singapore Slings, Dean. And how are you?"

"Excellent, Mr. West." Dean never forgot a customer. "How long are you in town for, Mr. West?"

"Search me. Until I finish my business, I suppose."

He took a seat across from Roy.

Roy called out, "No more for me, Dean. These are working hours. I'll nurse this one." To Julian he said, "I *was* in London. Boring job at a Reuters desk. All copy either from or to the States landed on it. I had to change Britishese into Americanese, and vice versa. You know, like calling gasoline 'petrol.' Anyway, it bored the hell out of me and when this hassle in Morocco started, I quit and came down to free-lance."

"What hassle?" Julian asked. He sipped his drink. "And what in the hell are all those people doing out in the streets?"

"There have been quite a few riots and demonstrations this last couple of weeks. The Moroccans want to bring the Sultan back—Mohammed the Fifth—and reunite the French Zone, and Spanish Zone, and the International Zone. The Sultan's in exile with about fifteen wives and concubines and about fifty servants and aides. My heart is really bleeding for him."

"Will they win?"

"Probably. Nobody wants colonies any more," Roy said cynically. "They're expensive to run, and it takes more to keep the people down than they're worth. The British didn't get out of India because they loved the Indians. It's more profitable to dominate a country by owning its industries, controlling its money, getting a monopoly on its trade and raw materials, than it is to own it. Even the French are finding that out. Meanwhile, though, they don't want to lose face. Last night, some of the Foreign Legion were brought into town. And the French have two tanks and several machine gun emplacements on the lawn of their embassy. Somebody will probably get hurt before the day's over. The rabble rousers are in the streets, trying to stir up a march on the French Embassy."

He nodded toward the door. "That's who's out there now—the potential mob. They're trying to get up their courage. Poor bastards, they don't have any weapons beyond cobblestones and clubs."

Julian took a tobacco pouch from his coat pocket and a Canadian shell briar, and loaded up. Silently, he picked up Roy's matches from the table and lit his pipe, exhaling through his nostrils.

Outside, the milling crowd was growing.

"First time I've ever seen a demonstration," Julian commented.

The newspaperman smiled wryly. "It probably won't be the last, the way the world's going. I'll try to cover the story when they get around to lining playboy entrepreneur Julian West up against the nearest wall for target practice.''

''They'll have to catch me first,'' Julian murmured, taking up his glass again.

Outside, the mob was moving. The French Embassy bordered the Place de France, only a long block away.

''There they go,'' said Roy. ''This business of yours in Tangier. Is there a story in it?''

Julian shrugged. ''I came to talk over a few things with Ira Levine, over at the Moses Periente bank. They handle some of the West Enterprises.''

''Moses Periente, eh?'' Roy looked thoughtful.

''What's wrong with Moses Periente? There's some talk of their moving their whole operation to Switzerland,'' Julian added.

Roy said carefully, ''The rumor in Tangier is that Moses Periente is going to move the operation all right, but to the Bahamas. And you know what that means. It's home base for every crooked financial operation in the world.''

''That wouldn't influence West Enterprises. We're too big to mess around with.''

At that moment there were two loud explosions from the direction of the French Embassy.

''Good God!'' Julian exclaimed. ''They're shelling the mob!''

Roy shook his head. ''No—not yet, at least. Those are noise bombs.''

''What in the hell's a noise bomb?''

''A bomb that makes a lot of noise but has no fragments. The riot police use them. It's a scare tactic.''

He rose to his feet, picked up his cigarettes from the table and put them into his pocket. "I'd better mosey on up and take a look."

"I'll come with you."

Roy stared at him for a couple of seconds. "This is the way I make my living. I *have* to go. . . ."

Julian banged his pipe out. He stood up, saying, "Put the drinks on my tab, Dean."

The bartender asked apprehensively, "Mr. London, do you think I ought to close up?"

"Yes," Roy responded laconically. He looked at Julian. "All right, sucker, let's go."

The street outside was comparatively empty now; those people to be seen were mostly women. They started up toward the plaza, in the direction of the mob.

In an alleyway stood some twenty soldiers with bayoneted rifles. They wore steel helmets, except the sergeant in charge who was bareheaded. His skull was shaven, deeply tanned with an ugly scar running from the top down to one mangled ear. He had cold, piercing eyes.

"French Legion," Roy muttered.

The sergeant growled in French, "Move on."

"Get screwed," Roy told him in English, but he was moving when he said it.

He turned to Julian. "They also brought in some water cannons last night. So all the fun and games won't be with noise bombs."

"What's a water cannon?"

They were nearing the square and the French Embassy. Julian could see two tanks within the iron fence which surrounded the building, the long cannon snoots pointed in the direction of the yelling, screaming demonstraters. There were quite a few legionnaires standing at ease on the Embassy lawn, with rifles or submachine guns in hand.

"Another anti-riot device, invented—surprise, surprise—in Germany. There's one up ahead," London said.

It looked like nothing so much as a gasoline truck, except that the windows were barred, and what appeared to be twin machine guns were mounted on top of the cab.

Roy slipped into a doorway and pulled Julian in beside him. "They shoot water at an unbelievable pressure, stronger than any firefighting equipment ever heard of. The next day the newspaper says, 'The police turned water on the mob and dispersed it.' Sounds innocuous to the reader, but it's deadly." Suddenly he grabbed Julian by the arm and hauled him deeper into their shelter. "Look out," he snapped.

A sizable element of the mob had spotted the vehicle and were running toward it, screaming in protest.

The two muzzles of the hoses atop the cab opened up and double streams of water, seemingly no thicker than a pencil, shot out.

The screams were suddenly cut off. The Moroccans were hurled back, smashed up against the brick building behind them, thrown to the sidewalk, tumbling and spilling driven back by the unbelievable pressure.

For a moment, a confused, terrified child stood alone. The water spray hit him before he could turn to run. It hit him at waist level and traversed his body, cutting him in two.

It was the child prostitute who had accosted Julian earlier.

Julian awoke in his bed in the high-rise apartment building of the University City. He was wringing with sweat.

Chapter Three

The Year 2, New Calendar

*The potentialities of science and technology for
the benefit of mankind as a whole are almost
inconceivably great, but the preparations which
we are making for their use and development are
pitiably small.*

— Lord Brain, *Science and Man*

WHEN JULIAN ENTERED the breakfast nook, the
three Leetes were already at the table but evidently
hadn't ordered yet. He was still somewhat shaken by
the nightmare. The child's death had been the most
horrible he had ever witnessed. And it couldn't have
been more useless. Within a month or so, the French
had capitulated and the Sultan, Mohammed V, had
returned to his throne. Much good it had done the
Moors.

They went through the standard morning greetings and Julian seated himself.

Doctor Leete said, "We put off deciding on breakfast until you joined us. I suggest we have Eggs à la Julian, your formula for shirred eggs that you introduced to us the other morning. Martha didn't have breakfast with us that day."

"Very well," Martha Leete agreed. "But only if Jule will submit to one of my recipes for lunch. I too am an amateur cook, Julian, with quite a few of my concoctions on file in the building's kitchen data banks." She made a move. "I wonder if anyone else ever orders them."

The doctor dialed the breakfast.

Edith asked, "Did you sleep well?"

"Very well," Julian lied.

"After slumbering over thirty years, beating Rip Van Winkle's record hands down, I'd think you'd never need to sleep again," she said, the sides of her mouth turning down in amusement.

All over again it came to him what an attractive young woman she was—and the fact that she would never be his. Their differences, no matter how small they might seem on the surface, were insurmountable.

The center of the table dropped down, to return with their breakfast. It was identically prepared to that of the other morning when he had first dictated the recipe into the kitchen data banks, and identically delicious.

"But this is wonderful," Martha exclaimed. "As I recall the food when I was a girl, it was on the grim side."

Julian thought about that as he ate. "I suppose that for every flow of tide, there's an ebb. It's true that back in the 1960s and '70s, food as a whole was deteriorating. But, in rebellion, there was an increasing number of people who were boycotting drive-in hamburger stands, cafeterias and so forth, and cooking their own would-be gourmet meals in their homes. All over the country, gourmet food stores, natural food farms and such were springing up. I used to know a chap who practically hand-raised beef. He fed the steers largely with mash saturated with beer, and kept them in stalls, never allowing them to graze. Every day, each steer was massaged. The beef produced was superlative. You had to buy a whole steer, which he had butchered for you, and you put it down in a deep freeze."

"It must have cost a fortune," Doctor Leete said.

"I imagine," Julian replied. "I wouldn't know. My chef used to pick it up. Price was no object." He looked over at the doctor's wife. "The grim food was eaten by those who couldn't afford such luxuries."

Edith said, a bit tartly, "Had you no qualms about eating the best while most of your countrymen——"

"None whatsoever. We of the elite believed that we deserved the best."

"Who decided you were the elite?" she inquired sarcastically.

"We did," he said, amused at her snide tone.

"Hmmm," Leete interjected. "The party roughens. Let's change the subject."

Julian put his fork down. "You know," he began, "my stay here with you has afforded me the epitome of hospitality, but it can't extend forever. I feel I am imposing. Isn't there some manner in which I could acquire quarters of my own, so I wouldn't be always under foot? A single room would be ample."

Leete chuckled. "There is already an apartment at your disposal, Julian. And it has been since you came out of hibernation. It is on the same floor as this one, and you can move in whenever you wish. Of course, there are no restraints upon you whatsoever. If you wish, you can move to some other area of the country, take a house or cottage—or even acquire a mobile home, if you like. However, it has been the earnest hope of the University that you would remain in residence for a time at least, for additional observation and later, perhaps, for some lectures about your experiences."

"It's wonderful here," Julian said quickly. "You've all been most kind. However, I *would* like my own quarters. But how do I pay for such an apartment.?"

"The rent is deducted from your Guaranteed Annual Income. As is everyone else's."

Julian frowned. "You mean, everybody pays the same rent, no matter how large the house or apartment?"

"Oh, no. The amount each citizen receives annually is large enough that he can do just about anything he wishes, but it is not infinite, obviously. Thus, some have larger apartments or homes than average, if that is what they particularly like. Others would rather spend less for rent, living in smaller quarters, and devote what they save to, say, travel—such places as Nepal, for mountain climbing, or Switzerland for skiing. Others are boating fans, possibly combined with such related sports as skin diving, fishing, water skiing and such. Some people, indeed, don't have apartments or houses at all, but live on boats for which they also must pay rent. Oh, there are many ways to spend your credits on things other than high rents."

"I see. Well, following breakfast, could you show me my apartment?" He added somewhat ruefully, "I won't have much packing to do. In fact, I'm all packed. Everything I own is in my pockets."

"Certainly." The doctor had finished his breakfast. He put down his utensils. "Why don't we go now?"

Julian West's quarters were only a short way down the corridor.

The doctor said, "It was thought that to be handy to us in this manner would enable you to easily check if anything comes up you don't understand. You are, of course, perfectly free to drop in on us at any time. My family is still assigned to adapting you to this new world."

"Very kind of you," Julian murmured.

Evidently the identity screen of the apartment had already been set to pick up his features; the door opened automatically at his approach.

He found the apartment more than satisfactory, though it gave him a somewhat impersonal feeling. He was going to have to work at locating some art objects, make a few changes in the furniture, acquire a differently colored rug.

While the doctor patiently sat in the living room which featured a window that composed the whole wall overlooking the university campus, Julian explored the place. Living room, bedroom, bath, small dining room, kitchenette complete with breakfast alcove, a study. The apartment was smaller than that of the Leetes, true, but amply spacious.

Exploration through, he returned to the living room and the doctor.

Leete came to his feet. "I'll leave you now so you can accustom yourself to your new h me. I assume you are fully acquainted with such matters as ordering from the kitchen and from the ultra-market, how to utilize the TV phone, and the National Data Banks library booster, your auto-teacher and so forth. But of course you are: you've been using them in my own apartment."

"Yes, certainly."

"Very well. Drop by as soon as you wish, my boy." The doctor smiled. "Imagine me calling you that. I find it hard to accept that you are older than I am."

Julian smiled too.

He left and for a moment, Julian wasn't sure that he didn't wish to follow Leete back to his apartment. Aside from the doctor, his wife, and Edith, Julian knew no one in this world. Or, at least, not in this part of it. There were surely past acquaintances throughout the country, who were still alive. By now they would be in their sixties, at least, and most in their seventies or more, but, sooner or later, he would get around to looking them up.

He could hardly have mentioned it to Leete, but his main reason for remaining in the Julian West University City was the fact that he was in love with Edith Leete. Though he had accepted that a permanent relationship with her was not possible, he still wanted to be near her, no matter how frustrating the contact.

He puttered around for a time, getting used to his new surroundings. The large window in the living room gave him the uncomfortable feeling of being in a goldfish bowl. He was on the fiftieth floor of the high-rise apartment building, however, and it was unlikely that anyone could see into his quarters. Then he noticed a dial at the side of the window. To his surprise, twisting it made the window go from completely clear to completely opaque. The day was superlative, so he returned it to transparency.

Well, his determination was to learn Interlingua as rapidly as possible. He entered the study and seated himself before the auto-teacher and activated it. In spite of everything that Edith and the others had said, he was going to make every effort to bring himself up to date at least to the point where he could communicate intelligently in this world of the year 2 New Calendar.

At that moment the door hummed.

He got up and went back into the living room. The door screen showed that it was Edith and someone he didn't know. He activated the door and greeted them.

The stranger was a young man in his mid-twenties who looked amazingly healthy and alert; tall, blond, Scandinavian in appearance. It occurred to Julian that all the young people he had seen since coming out of stasis were unbelievably fit looking. In a world where all received the best nourishment and the best of medical care from cradle to grave, he supposed the unattractive in appearance would be few indeed.

Edith smiled with her usual charm. "Julian, this is Sean Mathieson O'Callahan. He's a fellow student of anthropology."

The two men shook hands. "Well, now I know four persons in this era. Come in," said Julian.

He offered them seats.

"That's quite an imposing name you have," he said to the newcomer.

O'Callahan replied, "I think we've changed the method of naming since—since your time. We now follow the system the Spanish utilized. Sean, of course, is my given name. Mathieson is my father's name, and O'Callahan is my mother's. In short, descent is matrilineal, as it was through most of human history. It's based on the truism that it's a wise man who knows who his father is, but everyone knows his mother."

Edith laughed. "I told you he was an anthropologist."

Julian asked, "How is one named if the father isn't known?"

"We just use the mother's name then," O'Callahan said. "It's not particularly important. There is no such thing as illegitimacy."

"While we were waiting for you to come out of hibernation, we investigated your background, Jule," said Edith. "Your mother's name, maiden, was Van Hass, so by our usage your full name is Julian West Van Hass. Your parents were the famous jet set members, Barry and Betty—the Wild Wests, as they were called."

Julian nodded. "They were killed in a racing accident when I was quite young. I don't remember them too well. I didn't see much of them. I was usually in school, and they'd be off somewhere, father playing polo in the Argentine or participating in glider competitions in Austria, or the two of them winning automobile rallies in France. They earned their names ... the Wild Wests.''

''Something like Scott and Zelda?'' Edith asked.

He looked at her. ''I suppose so. You've read about the Fitzgeralds?''

''Yes, of course. I was always fascinated by their story. What a waste of talent when he died in his forties.''

''It wasn't wasted,'' Julian said. ''He simply burned himself out in a comparatively few years. Some of his contemporaries, such as Sinclair Lewis and possibly Hemingway and Steinbeck, wrote on after they should have stopped. My parents were friends of the Fitzgeralds and Hemingway. In fact, I knew Papa myself.''

''Zen!'' Sean exclaimed. ''Imagine having actually met Hemingway!''

''He was his own best character,'' Julian said.

Edith bent forward. ''You see why you are of such importance to us, Jule. You actually knew Hemingway. I understand he drank.''

He looked at her. ''Are you kidding?''

''That's what I mean,'' she said. ''You *knew* Hemingway. How recently did you see him?''

''Why about eight——'' He stopped, and there must have been something in his face.

Edith said quickly, ''Jule, Jule, I'm sorry.''

He changed the subject. ''Why aren't we speaking in Interlingua?''

Sean O'Callahan said somewhat shyly, ''If you

don't mind, I'd just as soon speak English. If you don't keep in practice with a language it falls away from you."

"You've studied English, then?"

"Yes, but not particularly so." He smiled in self-depreciation. "I learned it at home as a youngster. You see, my parents were die-hard conservatives. While the rest of the country was going all out to master the new international tongue, converting to the metric system, recycling their old gasoline automobiles, Mother and Dad struck stubbornly to English, and to inches, feet and miles, pints and quarts and all the rest of it, and they kept their overgrown Buick until it fell apart."

Edith laughed.

Sean said, "At any rate, although I learned Interlingua as soon as I attended school, we spoke English at home."

"Well," Julian told him, "since you're a guest, I give in. But I, too, need practice—in Interlingua."

Edith said, "I brought Sean over since Father thinks you should be meeting more of our contemporaries. And Sean has been nagging me since you were first revived."

Julian nodded. "It's just as interesting for me to meet you. By your appearance, I assume you were born while I was still in stasis."

"Yes, I am twenty-six years of age."

"Oh, then you had your first Muster Day last year, as I understand the institution. The day when the computers either select you for some job . . . or don't."

The younger man was rueful. "Didn't, in my case.

My field is history, archaeology, and anthropology. The need for teachers and field workers is rather minimal. I wasn't chosen by the Aptitude Quotient computers. I'll keep working away at it as a student but I rather doubt if I will ever be selected for a job. When only two percent of the population can do all the necessary work, you don't have much of a chance. This year, only a couple of dozen graduates were selected from our university city to go into the field of archaeology.''

Julian shook his head. ''Tough luck. It's directly opposite from my time. In those days, most people who could get out of work did so. Under this socioeconomic system, with everyone trained in the field they like best, you practically all *want* to work and there is no need for you.''

''That's right,'' Sean said, his voice still rueful. Then, ''Do you mind if I ask you some questions, Mr. West?''

''Julian, or better still, Jule. Certainly you may, if you grant me the same privilege. Fire away.''

''You were in Vietnam, weren't you?''

''Yes, I was.''

''A combat soldier?''

Julian nodded cautiously. Like most combat men, he didn't particularly like to recall his experiences. He had found long since that those who talked most about military action had usually seen the least.

Sean pulled at the lobe of his right ear. ''As an historian, it fascinates me.''

Julian frowned. ''But the Vietnam War ended only a bit over thirty years ago. There must be a good many veterans among your older people. A man who

35

was your age in the latter Vietnam years would only be in his mid-fifties or so now.''

But the other shook his head. "After thirty years you don't remember actual events with a great deal of accuracy. In fact, some authorities claim that after a quarter of a century you usually don't have correct memory at all, but only memories of memories. I have talked to a good many soldiers but not very satisfactorily. But you . . . for you it is as though it happened just the other day. In your memory, how long has it been since you were in action?''

"A few months," Julian replied uncomfortably. Now that he thought about it, Doctor Leete had told him much the same thing.

Edith put in hurriedly, "I am afraid the conversation is upsetting you, Jule. Father wants you to avoid emotional disturbances at this stage of your recovery.''

"It's all right," Julian said, looking at Sean. "What did you want to know?''

"You can still do such things as fire a machine gun accurately, throw a grenade, fight with a bayonet. . . ?''

"In Vietnam there was precious little bayonet fighting. Possibly in the First World War, in the trenches, but by Vietnam the bayonet was more or less antiquated. Grenades? There's not much to know about grenades. You pull the pin and heave, or, if you need more distance, you attach a grenade launcher to the end of your rifle. A machine gun? Yes, I could field strip a machine gun in complete darkness, or a .45 automatic, for that matter. Could I still fire one accurately? Yes. I was an averagely good marksman.''

"What rank did you hold . . . Julian?"

"I was discharged a major."

The other was leaning forward. "Excuse me, but . . . well, did you ever kill anyone?"

Julian took a breath. "Yes."

"How many?"

He shook his head. "I don't know. I haven't the vaguest idea. You see, in modern warfare—I suppose I should say in the Vietnam War, rather than use the term 'modern'—combat doesn't much resemble the war films you have possibly scanned from the data banks. Hollywood didn't make movies that portrayed reality; they would be too boring. In the movies, the action is eyeball to eyeball, with the bad guys—the Germans, Japs, Koreans, Viet Cong, or whoever—falling like flies before the good guys who are armed with submachine guns that never run out of ammo and never heat up, no matter how many hundreds of rounds go through the barrels in a few minutes. In actuality, you see comparatively little of the enemy, although there are some exceptions. Fire power is all the thing. You fire in the general direction of where his fire is coming from. You put as much lead and steel into the air as you can, hoping that Charlie will run into it. You saturate the area he is in with bullets, with mortar shells, with artillery shells, with bombs from your air cover. And then, when all is quiet and Charlie is either dead or, more likely, has largely slipped away, you go forward and get a body count."

"A body count?" Edith said. In spite of herself, her face was registering that she was upset.

Julian looked at her. "Yes. It was a return to the barbarism of Indian warfare days. To prove how many of the enemy we had killed, we cut off their ears and took them back to base headquarters."

"Proof of the number you had destroyed, eh?" Sean asked, fascinated.

Julian took another quick breath. "Yes. But the thing is, the Colonel, and the General above him, liked to have an impressive body count, so we customarily also cut the ears off any women, children, or old men that had managed to get in the line of fire or bombing."

"But those were civilians," Edith said in horror.

"Right," Julian agreed, his tone sour. "But we couldn't allow that to interfere with a good body count." He scowled at Sean. "Did you labor under the illusion that combat was glamorous?"

The other didn't respond. Instead he asked, "Were you ever afraid when you were fighting?"

"I was always afraid when I was fighting," Julian said flatly. "Anybody in combat who doesn't get afraid—the hero type, in short—isn't the kind of man you want next to you. He's one of the crazies and is apt to get you in trouble."

That set the student of history back a bit. He asked his next question more hesitantly, "Did you ever do anything that resulted in your being decorated, getting a medal?"

Julian grunted. "I was awarded the Distinguished Service Cross, also several battle stars and three Purple Hearts." A muscle jumped in his jaw and he looked into Edith's face almost apologetically. "I didn't ask for them. After two or three weeks in the rice paddies and the jungles, I did not ask for those things. But it was meaningless to refuse them—

particularly the Purple Hearts."

"Purple Hearts?" she echoed.

"Yes. You received one for being wounded."

Her eyes rounded.

He shrugged it off. "Routine stuff. Once I was hit by a piece of mortar shell while sitting in a foxhole minding my own business. Once I stepped on a homemade Viet Cong mine. It didn't go off very efficiently or I wouldn't be here. The other time I was hit by an M-16 rifle slug from one of my own men. It was an accident . . . I think. Toward the end of the war, quite a few officers took hits from their men, if they seemed to be too gung ho. Not that I was."

"Gung ho?" Sean said. He had been taking notes in a small black notebook with a stylo.

"Anxious to win the war," Julian explained dryly. "Officers who would try to get their men into situations the men didn't like the looks of."

"But I thought you had to obey an officer's orders."

"Yes, that was the theory. But it wasn't a very popular war and the men wanted to live long enough to go home. Nobody seemed to know why we were fighting except the politicians back in Washington. Toward the end, morale was so bad among the infantry that it was impossible to remain in Vietnam, which was one of the real reasons we pulled out, rather than the propaganda reasons the people were given." He stopped. "Why are you taking notes, Sean?"

The younger man flushed. "When I was turned down as a teacher, I decided that one way to be active in the work I like is to become a journalist. I plan to do as many articles as I can on developments in the fields I know and submit them to the news. If enough readers dial my articles, I may be able to become a full-time journalist. I'd rather teach, but since my Aptitude Quotient wasn't high enough, journalism might be the next best thing."

"I wish you luck, Sean," Edith said. She took her transceiver from her pocket and touched the stud for the time. "My goodness, sirs," she exclaimed. "I'll have to run. I have an appointment." She rose with a degree of grace that didn't go unnoticed.

Julian had also started to stand, but she grimaced at him playfully. "None of that male chauvinism courtesy," she said. "I don't stand for you, why should you for me?"

"I was going to see you out."

"Why? I can find my own way to the door and you're still talking to Sean."

"As you wish," he said in resignation. "I'll see you later, Edie."

"Fine. Is there anything you need that we haven't checked you out on as yet?"

"I can't think of anything."

She looked about the room. "This place is on the grim side. Why don't you dial Art, in the data banks, and select some paintings?"

"I was going to ask you about that. Can I afford them?"

"The price is minimal."

He said unhappily, "I imagine modern art is pretty far out. Frankly, my tastes never developed beyond the Impressionists."

Edith practically snorted. "With some twenty

million painters in the country, every school that ever existed, from the Cro-Magnon cave painters to the present, is represented. You'll find all the Impressionists you want in the painting banks.''

"Twenty million painters?" he repeated blankly.

Both Sean and Edith laughed.

Edith said, "I don't really know the exact number. I told you that just about everyone in United America has at least one art or handicraft as a hobby, beyond whatever type of work he specializes in. Well, until later. . . . Good-bye, Sean."

The young man waved farewell to her, and she turned and left.

Julian looked back at Sean. "Anything more you want to know about blood and guts?"

"Not at the moment." The other put away his notebook and stylo. "But I'd appreciate the opportunity to talk with you more when I've digested what you've told me and thought up some more questions."

"Anytime. I'll probably have a few to ask you, as well. I seem to have done most of the talking today."

Sean hesitated for a moment. "You know, I have some friends who would love to meet you too. Do you think you could sneak away from Doctor Leete and his family some evening?"

"Sneak away?"

Sean laughed, in some embarrassment. He said, "Leete's been given the job of adjusting you to your new environment, and it's well known that he's keeping you on a tight rein. It frustrates some of the rest of us who would love to have the chance to talk with a man who has actually been in combat—just a few months ago, in his mind—who has witnessed riots in the streets of the nineteen-sixties, who remembers clearly the days of street crime, juvenile delinquency, and all the rest of it.''

Julian smiled. ''I didn't think of the good doctor as my jailer, but I suppose in a way he is. How could we get together?''

''Why don't we meet down on the ground level in the Cub Bar?''

''Cub Bar?''

''I suppose thus far the Leetes haven't taken you out to any of the public places of entertainment. It's a pleasant, intimate little bar, one of several dozen in this building. Could you meet me there, say, tonight at eight?''

''Certainly,'' Julian said, standing as the other did. ''I'd like to see the present-day equivalent of a bar. And I'm anxious to meet more of the present generation. Will they speak English too? My Interlingua isn't all that good.''

''They'll speak English.''

Julian saw him to the door. After Sean was gone, he thought of one question he could have asked. How did one go about getting a girl to sleep with him in this day and age?

Chapter Four

The Year 2, New Calendar

Despite the perils and problems of our times, we should be glad that we are living in this age. Every civilization is like a surf rider, carried forward on the crest of a wave. The wave bearing us has scarcely started its run; those who thought it was already slackening spoke centuries too soon. We are poised now, in the precarious but exhilarating balance that is the essence of real living, the antithesis of mere existence. Behind us lie the reefs we have already passed; beneath us the great wave, as yet barely flecked with foam, humps its back from the sea. . . . . And ahead. . .? We cannot tell; we are too far out to see the unknown land. It is enough to ride the wave.

— Arthur C. Clarke,
Profiles of the Future

WHEN HE WAS once again alone, Julian moved about the apartment, checking it out in more detail. So far as he could see, there was no reason in the world why he couldn't be comfortable here. It was smaller than the apartment he had maintained in the United Nations Plaza building in New York, or even the Paris place on the Left Bank, but he wasn't going to need servants here; Edith had explained that the apartments were entirely automated. He was going to have to check that one out. How the hell could you automate sweeping, dusting, washing windows; above all, how could you automate making a bed? Not that he couldn't make his own bed, of course.

It was too early in the day, but he decided he could use a drink. He went back into the living room, to the small auto-bar which stood in one corner. He stared down at it. Although he had been in the Leete home for some time now, he had never used the auto-bar in their apartment; someone else had always gotten the drinks.

Well, it couldn't be too complicated. There was a numbered dial and also a button, below a speaker. Experimentally, he pressed the button. He hadn't the vaguest idea how to dial. Probably, somewhere around here, there was a pamphlet listing drinks, and all you had to do was dial what you wanted.

Instead, he cleared his throat and said, "I'd like a martini, with a twist of lemon peel rather than an olive."

A slightly mechanical voice answered, "We are sorry, Mr. West, but that beverage is not on our list."

He was genuinely surprised. "A *martini* not on your list?"

"No, Mr. West. However, if you will give us the formula it shall be placed in the building's data banks."

"All right. You take four, no make that five parts of gin and put it in a shaker with one part dry vermouth and lots of ice. You stir it briskly until it is very cold, but not too long so that too much of the ice melts. You pour it into a pre-chilled, thin-shelled cocktail glass and then twist a peel of lemon over it and drop the peel into the drink.''

''Thank you, Mr. West. The formula is now on file.''

He stood back half a step and scowled at the auto-bar. Now what?

It couldn't have been two minutes before the top of the bar sank down to rise up again with a highly chilled, champagne-size glass. He was somewhat taken aback. He should have told them just what he meant by a part; that is, about a third of an ounce. There were at least five ounces of gin in this over-sized, so-called cocktail glass. Well, he could straighten that out with them later. He took the drink and went over to the easy chair that was placed before the room's TV screen.

He got out the screen's directory and looked up the General News. Then he dialed it.

If he understood correctly, General News was the equivalent of the front page in the papers of his own day. Front page and possibly second and third.

The material began flashing before him, but it was Interlingua, and he was incapable of understanding more than one word out of three. He dialed for Information and asked it he could have the General News in English.

No problem, except that he couldn't follow it even in English. It was too technical, except for a few items on entertainment and social matters. In disgust, he dialed again and, with a slight rasp in his voice, asked for the news in English for younger people—between the ages of eight and ten.

The voice said, "Of course, Mr. West."

"What do you mean, *of course?*" he snarled.

"Yes, sir," the voice said unemotionally, as always.

How the hell did you argue with a computer? He settled back in the chair and took an irritated pull at his martini. Even the computers in this building knew that he had the educational level of a ten-year-old—maybe less.

For he found his work cut out for him trying to follow along even on that level.

The news was considerably different than it had been a third of a century ago. For one, there was no crime news. He was to find out later that this came under the heading of Medical News, and there was precious little of it. There was no financial news, either, which was one of the first items he used to look up in the *Times* and the *Wall Street Journal*.

There was a good deal of scientific and technological news, practically all of it entirely beyond him.

"Good God, this is for eight-year-olds?" he muttered, pulling at his overgrown martini again.

There was a great deal of sports; but there had been changes. There was no longer such a thing as boxing, although there was wrestling, and no karate or judo. There was seemingly no bullfighting, or auto racing, or any other sport that might involve someone getting hurt. There wasn't even football. The remnants of the Roman arena had disappeared from the sports scene, and viewers of spectacle sports evidently no longer got their kicks from the fact that they might witness a serious injury, or even death. Nobody got hurt in the sports of this era.

There was a great deal of entertainment news. Some of it was on a new order for him. For instance, it would seem that one of the current entertainment fads involved composing poems—*on your feet*. That is, a contestant would be given, cold, a subject, and within only a few minutes, he was expected to deliver his poem. The judges would give him both the subject and a verse form—a sonnet, or more intricate French form such as a rondeau—and he would have to compose in that form and on that subject. There was no possible manner in which he could prepare himself beforehand. In such a contest, Julian decided, he would have considered that he'd done well if he were able to come up with anything:

> Cold Beer
> Sold Here

It would seem that in this age, intellectual exercises were all the thing. He wondered if they still played charades. Back in the fifties, he had rather prided himself on his own abilities. If the game had become extinct, he would reintroduce charades.

He gave up on the General News and tried, in the way of an experiment, Music. In his day he had been exposed to classical music beyond the point of desire, but it was a social must. These people now seemed to live for it. A musical great was the equivalent in status of a billionaire in his own time.

Ballet followed Music. There seemed to be a ballet revival that would have given Nijinsky and Pavlova back seats. He had always liked ballet. He wondered if they ever did the old classics, such as Swan Lake.

But Scientific News was half of all news, and he was lost. Even in English on the ten-year-old level, he hadn't the vaguest idea of what he was reading. He abruptly flicked off the set, picked up his glass and finished off his martini. He slumped back in this chair, thoroughly frustrated. He didn't know enough in this day even to know where to begin.

He flicked the screen back on, for something had occurred to him.

He dialed information and said, "I want a resume, in English, on an eight- to ten-year level, on the outstanding scientific breakthroughs that have taken place since the year 1970 Old Calendar."

"Yes, Mr. West. That will take two or three minutes to compile. Did you wish an extensive report or a brief?"

He suspected that an extensive report would take him the better part of the rest of the week to wade through. "Just a brief."

Two or three minutes. It was the first time the International Data Banks hadn't come back with something he wanted immediately. Probably it was the first time the request had ever been made. He shrugged and settled back in his chair.

While he waited, he thought back over his conversation with Edith and Sean O'Callahan. He hadn't really told them anything about combat. Not really. It wasn't something easy to tell about; you almost had to witness it to understand. Oh, some of the really good writers had been able to tell it true. Wasn't that the way Hemingway had said it, *tell it true?* Something like that. But the Old Man had been there, and more than once. Papa Hemingway had been one of the few men Julian West had ever met who actually seemed to like war.

Johnny Reston came back to him now. Sergeant John Reston. They had been a team for some six months down in the Mekong Delta area. They had worked out a system, based on that of pursuit pilots. Johnny acted as the equivalent of a wing man for Julian; that is, he remained to the right and a few yards behind him when they went into action. Julian was the point man and directed his fire at the enemy. Johnny spent full time covering him, ignoring offensive action of his own, unless it involved protecting his buddy. It had worked pretty well until the day when they were wading waist deep in water, wading desperately for dry land and cover, that an exploding mortar shell hit Johnny almost dead center. A great deal of blood and gore that had been Sergeant John Reston was flung over Julian. After he had gotten to land, he had vomited his guts out.

Yes, he could have told Sean and Edith about that. But could he have told it true, as Papa had demanded? Probably not; he could never have brought home to them the reality of the thing, the nauseating horror. As he recalled, it had only been a week later that he stepped on the land mine and nearly had his leg blown off. Two months in hospital and, when he had recovered, he had two weeks' R & R in Bangkok where he picked up the only case of venereal disease he had ever experienced.

The screen lit up before him and he began to scan the developments in science since the time Doctor

Herbert Pillsbury had put him into stasis.

SCIENTIFIC AND TECHNOLOGICAL BREAKTHROUGHS SINCE 1970— NOT NECESSARILY IN ORDER OF DISCOVERY

1. *Applications of masers and lasers for sensing, communication, measuring, heating, cutting, power transmission, mining and illumination, and other purposes.*

Well, the Leetes had already told him a bit about that, although he still didn't understand what in the hell a laser was. He vaguely remembered reading somewhere that it was a very narrow beam of light, and had the potential to be made into a death ray.

2. *Very high-temperature and high-strength structural materials. New and improved fabrics such as fibers, papers, and plastics and new materials for appliances and equipment such as alloys, glasses, ceramics, intermetallics, and cermets.*

3. *New sources of power for fixed installations such as magnetohydrodynamic, thermoelectric, thermoionic and radioactivity, and new sources of power for transportation including improved storage batteries, fuel cells, propulsion by electric-magnetic fields and jet engines.*

All right, that was to be expected. He had missed a couple of the words. What were cermets, and what was magnetohydrodynamic? He supposed he should order a dictionary from the ultra-market down in the basement. Right now that would slow him up too much, however, looking up every word he didn't understand.

4. *Worldwide use of high-altitude cameras in satellites for weather control, mapping, geological investigations, prospecting, and land use.*

5. *New methods of water transport, including automated cargo ships, hovercraft, submarine carriers pulled by surface tugs, and developments in container ships. Ground Effect Machines, eliminating the need to load and unload cargo at sea ports.*

Nothing startling there, either. All of it had been germinating in his own time. But the next one set him back.

6. *Advances in cyborg techniques such as substitutes or mechanical aids for limbs, senses, or organs.*

Dr. Leete had told him that they no longer transplanted organs. Did he, Julian West, have an artificial heart in his chest?

7. *New techniques and institutions for education, including chemical methods for improving learning and memory, and home education via video and computerized programmed learning.*

He knew about that, too—and that it largely applied only to youth.

8. *New and improved materials and equipment for buildings including variable transmission glass, heating and cooling by thermoelectric effect, and phosphorescent and electroluminescent lighting.*

9. *Widespread use of cryogenics.*

He hadn't any idea as to cryogenics and could only guess at electroluminescent lighting.

10. *Recoverable boosters for space launching, direct broadcasts from satellites to home receivers, permanent lunar bases, manned satellites and planetary bases, and the beginnings of planetary engineering.*

Most of that had been in the cards when he went into hibernation, although he didn't know what they meant by planetary engineering.

11. *High-capacity, worldwide, regional, and local communication through satellites, light pipes and lasers, and video TV communications, including tape material from data banks and rapid transmission of facsimilies including news, library material, instantaneous mail delivery, and other printouts.*

12. *Large scale desalinization through use of nuclear fusion and solar power, allowing for reforestation of such areas as the Sahara.*

13. *Widespread use of computers for intellectual assistance, including translation, teaching, literature search, medical diagnosis, traffic control, computation, design analysis, and other functions.*

14. *Transceivers for personal communication on a worldwide basis.*

15. *Stimulated, planned, and programmed dreams.*

That last one set him back again. He was going to have to ask the doctor about that.

16. *Extensive genetic control regarding humans, animals, and plants.*

He refused to think about that for the time.

17. *Artificial growth of new limbs and organs, either in situ or for later transplantation.*

Another one to ask the doctor about.

18. *Indefinite suspended animation.*

He was on home ground with that one. Indefinite? He had been under for more than thirty years, hadn't he? Now, he supposed, new developments had occurred.

19. *Major rejuvenation and significant extention of life span and vigor.*

That was something! He wondered to what extent. Somebody—Edith, he thought—had already told him that man was no longer tied to his traditional three score years and ten.

20. *Automated highways and moving sidewalks for local transportation.*

21. *Substantial progress toward anti-gravity.*

22. *Lifetime immunization against practically all diseases.*

23. *Understanding of cetacean languages.*

That would mean communication with . . . well, porpoises, whales, and dolphins, wouldn't it?

24. *Wireless energy——*

Before he could finish taking it in, his TV phone hummed. He switched off his auto-teacher screen and activated the phone. It was Edith.

"Have you forgotten that you promised to have lunch with us? Mother was to present one of her recipes."

He said, "Sorry, Edie. I was all caught up in research. I'll be right over."

The Leete door opened at his approach, it too being keyed in to his face. He went on into the living room where both Edith and her mother were already at the dining room table.

Martha smiled at him. "I've already dialed for

lunch. I hope you like Oysters Diablo.''

He took his customary place. ''I'm an oyster man from way back but I don't believe I know that dish.'' He looked around. ''Isn't the doctor going to be with us? I've managed to accumulate some more questions about the changes that have taken place since my times.''

Mrs. Leete frowned slightly. ''I can't imagine where he is. He went out a short time ago on an errand that should have taken but a few minutes. Perhaps something came up. We can start without him.''

It was then that the living room door opened and Doctor Leete stumbled in. His clothes were rumpled and soiled, blood trickled from the side of his mouth, and one of his eyes was swollen.

The three at the table were on their feet instantly.

''Raymond!'' Martha screamed.

Julian hurried to the side of the doctor. ''What in the hell happened?'' he asked as he led the older man to a couch.

Edith was at her father's side, eyes wide. ''Father! What on earth happened?''

Doctor Leete brought a handkerchief from his pocket and dabbed at his mouth. He was gasping for breath.

He said, as though he couldn't believe it himself, ''I . . . I was just mauled by three young men in the elevator.''

''Mauled!'' Martha Leete was next to her husband, her hand anxiously on his arm.

Julian had gone to the auto-bar. He came back with a stiff shot of brandy. ''Here,'' he said. ''I know you don't ordinarily drink, but you look as though you could use this. I thought you didn't have juvenile delinquency any more. What did they take?"

The doctor looked at him blankly. "Take? What could they take? I have nothing worth taking. We don't have money. Nobody wears jewelry. I have nothing anybody else couldn't get by simply dialing the ultra-markets."

Edith said, "But . . . I've never heard of such a thing. . . . I've never heard of physical violence taking place in this building."

Julian was the only one present familiar with such matters. He asked, "What did they do?"

The doctor shook his head, as though to clear it. "They got into the elevator with me. As we ascended, one suddenly struck me with his fist in the abdomen. Then the others began to hit me. That's all I can remember, except . . . one thrust his hand into my jacket pocket."

"For what?"

The doctor shook his head again, his breath coming more naturally now. "For nothing. There was nothing there."

Martha said in bewilderment, "But this doesn't make sense, Raymond. You have no enemies."

Her husband put his hand in his jacket pocket, as though to demonstrate that there was nothing in it. Then he frowned. He withdrew a slip of paper and scowled at it. When he had read it, he shook his head in confusion.

Julian took the slip from him. *When a social revolution is pending and, for whatever reason, is not accomplished, reaction is the alternative. At such a time any reform measures proposed are concealed measures of reaction — Daniel DeLeon*. He handed the note to Martha Leete. She and Edith read it, both looking bewildered.

"Who in the hell's Daniel DeLeon?" Julian asked.

The doctor had caught his breath by now. He said, mystified, "Was, not is. He was a revolutionist about 1900. Very prominent in socialist circles a century ago."

Julian looked at Edith. "Can't you call the police?"

"We don't have police, in the old sense of the word," she said, standing. "But I'll call University Security."

But something strange had come over the doctor's face. He took the note back from his wife and reread it, then looked up and shook his head. "No, don't do that. I want to think about this."

And now Edith had a thoughtful look too.

She turned to Julian. "Jule, I'm sorry, but would you mind? It doesn't look as though a very pleasant lunch is in the offing."

"There's nothing I can do?"

It was the doctor who answered him. "No. No, Julian. I'll be all right. We'll see you later."

Chapter Five

The Year 2, New Calendar

No society is eager for its own dissolution and all societies try—instinctively, as it were—to perpetuate the status quo.
            —Margaret Halsey, *The Corrupted Giant*

AS BEWILDERED AS the Leetes, Julian returned to his own apartment. They had told him that crime had disappeared in this so-called Republic of the Golden Rule, that there were no more juvenile delinquents, that muggings were a thing of the past. Who in the name of whatever might be holy, would want to beat up kindly old Doctor Leete?

He had no frame of reference in which to consider

the problem. He gave it up and went into his kitchenette, to the little breakfast nook there. Hesitating momentarily, he dialed Information and asked for a ham sandwich and a bottle of beer.

Had it been possible for a computer voice to register a tone of surprise, it undoubtedly would have.

"Would you repeat that order, Mr. West?"

He repeated it, then said, impatiently, "You take two pieces of bread and butter each lightly on one side. You put between them a slice of ham, moderately thick, covered lightly with mustard, along with some lettuce. You serve it with a dill pickle."

"Yes, Mr. West. We shall put the recipe in the kitchen data banks. But we do not serve beer in bottles, sir."

"Well, serve it any damn way you wish," he said.

"Very well, Mr. West."

Shortly, the table sank down to return with his order. The beer was in a large glass and by the looks of the thick, rich head, it was draft. There was too much lettuce. He removed half of it and ate.

After lunch, there was nothing else he could think of to do so he went back to his study. He resumed his seat before the auto-teacher and took up his studies of Interlingua where he had left off.

In his determination to master the language as quickly as possible, so that he could get on with his studies—albeit on a grammar school level—he stuck to it with all the concentration he could muster, knocking off only twice to get himself a drink from the auto-bar.

To his surprise, when he checked the time he found that it was pushing eight o'clock, and then it came back to him that he had a date with young O'Callahan in the Cub Bar. Well, he was tired of studying. The break would be a relief.

He had heard no more from the Leetes, so he assumed that they were through with him for the day. They had enough on their minds not to want their charge underfoot. He deactivated his auto-teacher and left the apartment, taking the elevator down to the ground floor.

He looked about the huge, Grecian-style lobby, wondering where the Cub Bar might be.

A bright young thing, done up in the usual coveralls which seemed to be the most popular garb for either sex, came up to him and said in Interlingua, "May I help you? You're Mr. West, aren't you?"

He said haltingly, in the same language, "Why, yes. Thank you. I was looking for the Cub Bar."

"The Cub Bar is just down there. At the end of that corridor. It's fascinating to meet you, Mr. West."

She was looking at him smilingly, as though expecting him to say something further, but all he could think of was, "Thank you, very much."

She looked disappointed, turned and left. He watched her go, feeling somehow inadequate, but he didn't know why.

The Cub Bar, it turned out, had little to bear out its name, so far as the bars with which he had been familiar with in the past were concerned. And he had been familiar with a good many.

About all it had in common with the places he remembered was rather dim light. There was no bar, complete with barman, at which one could sit. There was no jukebox, thank God, although there was very faint background music issuing from somewhere he couldn't determine. There were booths and there were tables, and the walls were tastefully done with paintings, largely representational, and very beautiful tapestries.

He located Sean O'Callahan, or, rather, the archaeology-history student located him and was waving. Julian made his way over to the booth. Two others were seated with him, both of them older men, in their fifties or early sixties.

Sean stood at his approach, looking more pleased than Julian thought was called for.

He slid into the booth and waited for the introductions. He had rather expected the persons Sean O'Callahan had wanted him to meet to be contemporaries of the younger man.

Sean said, "Julian West Van Hass, may I introduce William Dempsey Harrison and Frederic Madison Ley."

On a quick sizing-up, Harrison emanated energy and even aggression, a stocky, confident type in excellent physical shape for his years. Ley reminded him more of the movie star of yesteryear, a sleepy, otherwise expressionless look about his face. His body had just slightly gone to flab. Even before he spoke, Julian was of the opinion that he wasn't much given to talk.

They shook hands, went through the usual amenities, then Harrison, with a quick wave of his hand to indicate their three glasses, said, "We've already ordered. What would you like?"

To his surprise, Harrison and Ley obviously had

highballs of one sort or another. Only Sean had a beer glass before him.

Julian asked for Scotch and soda, and Harrison, who seemed to be senior member of the team, put his transceiver in the payment slot of the table and dialed for it.

Ley drawled, "Yeah, we used to drink a lot of Scotch in the old days. It's mostly belly-wash they drink now."

Julian's drink came. He raised his glass by way of a toast. "Sean tells me that I'm quite a freak, what with being a war veteran and all."

Ley said quickly, "I was in 'Nam."

Harrison looked at him. "Yes, but it was a long time ago, wasn't it?"

The other lapsed into silence. It was obvious that he deferred to the aggressive Harrison.

Sean beamed. He was pleased with his success in pulling off this gathering.

Harrison stared at Julian West for a long moment. "We've been hearing about you on the News for a long time. You know, of those who went into hibernation, you're the first to be awakened. And nobody else was put under for something like ten years after you volunteered."

"So I understand," Julian said easily. "But I didn't exactly volunteer. No old soldier ever volunteers. With me, it was a matter of going into stasis, or dropping dead in my tracks at any moment."

Harrison nodded. "At any rate, you're the one person around who really remembers the old days."

"I remember them," Ley growled.

Harrison didn't even look at him. "You were a kid," was all he said.

He leaned back to observe Julian some more. He seemed to come to some conclusion. "What do you think of our present socioeconomic system, Mr. West, after several weeks with us?" There was a cautious note in his voice that Julian couldn't quite understand.

"Why, I suppose it's the nearest thing to Utopia that the race has ever achieved."

Harrison said carefully, "There have been other 'near Utopias,' you know."

Julian took another pull at his drink. "It's not my field, but. . . . An example?"

Harrison put his elbows on the table and tented his fingertips. In a somewhat condescending manner he replied, "Ancient Egypt, for instance."

Julian laughed a little. "Oh come now, you're putting me on. Say 'Ancient Egypt' to me and the first picture that flashes to mind is an overseer with a whip giving it to a dozen slaves who are pushing an over-sized cut stone along on rollers for a half-finished pyramid in the background. That's Utopia?"

The other waggled a finger at him. "There are a good many misconceptions, even among anthropologists, about the early dynasties of Egypt. The Pharaoh was not a king, Mr. West, and the people were not slaves. Later, things were to change—please keep that in mind—but the early Pharaohs, both of the Upper and Lower so-called kingdoms, were the equivalent of tribal chieftains, elected by the clan elders. And slavery had not evolved as yet. The people were comparatively free and their institutions democratic. The clan elders were elected by the clansmen; they were not hereditary. Even Menes, the Pharaoh who is accredited with uniting Upper and Lower Egypt, was not a monarch but a revered war chief and high priest. At this stage, the Egyptians as a people maintained a surprising standard of living as compared to the rest of the world. Considering that nine-tenths of the human race at the time were wearing animal skins— the Egyptians already had cotton—and surviving as best they could in a Neolithic hunting-and-gathering economy, Egypt was a Utopia indeed. It was after the first ten dynasties or so that the democratic institutions eroded, at least in part, and the clan chiefs became hereditary, as did the Pharaohs. Slavery was introduced, though to a lesser degree than is usually supposed. The everyday Egyptian was not a slave beaten with whips.''

Julian was out of his depth. Wondering how in the hell the conversation had taken this bent, he commented, ''Well, I suppose a case could be made for what you say. I suppose it's a comparative thing— Utopia. Undoubtedly, a thousand years from now our descendants will look upon this period and consider us semi-barbarians.''

''Possibly, if this present socioeconomic system continues, Mr. West.''

Julian sipped his drink and frowned at the other questioningly. Harrison didn't seem particularly interested in his drink, nor did Sean or the dour Ley.

Harrison said, ''The pyramids of Gizeh, the greatest constructions of antiquity, were built during the Fourth Dynasty, roughly 2700 B.C. So was the

Sphinx, one of the most noble pieces of sculpture ever produced. In this early Utopia of ours, art was well established. The point I was building up to is that three thousand years were to pass without any fundamental changes in Egyptian art, its sciences, its technology; in short, its way of life. There was seemingly no need for change. The Nile fed them abundantly, their clothing needs were minimal, as were their housing needs in that climate. They had it made, so to speak. Oh, there were ups and downs on the political scene. For about a hundred years the Hyksos, the so-called shepherd-kings, ruled them, and at another point the black Nubians took over. But these conquerors didn't basically change the socioeconomic system. It was still a comparatively stilted Utopia for the average Egyptian. It wasn't until the coming of the Greeks under Alexander and the progressive rule of the Ptolemies that Egypt began to break out of the cocoon in which she had existed for three millennia.''

"I see," Julian said, not seeing at all. "And another example of Utopia in the past?''

Harrison thought for a moment, finally taking a sip of his drink.

"The Mayans, perhaps. They were on the scene possibly as early as 1500 B.C. One of their first cities, Tikal, in Guatemala, is also one of their most impressive. The temple of the Jaguar God is over one-hundred sixty feet, one of the highest and most beautiful of Mayan pyramids. Early in the game they reached an astonishingly advanced level of mathematics, having hit upon the zero many centuries before the Europeans had it; likewise in astronomy, in medicine, in architecture and other arts. As in the case of the Egyptians, they too had it made. Guatemala, Chiapas, and Yucatan are lush. Actually, the Mayans ate better than the Spanish at the time of the conquest. They, like the early Egyptians, had a tribal society, perhaps top-heavy with the priesthood, but the people were free. Slavery, as we know it, was unknown. Their fabulous pyramids, temples, and governmental buildings, such as the House of the Governors in Uxmal, were built by communal labor, during the months of the year not needed for agricultural work. It was, Mr. West, a Neolithic Utopia." He paused and, without asking, dialed another Scotch for Julian.

"And so?" Julian prodded. He couldn't get the drift. Sean had said these friends had wanted to talk about firsthand accounts of the mid-twentieth century. But here he was getting a rundown on ancient history.

Harrison went on. "One of their last cities, built shortly before the coming of the Spanish, was Mayapan. Mr. West, it was little, if at all, more advanced than Tikal. More than a thousand years earlier they had achieved a calendar more accurate than our own Gregorian, and had hit upon the zero, but where were their *new* advances? They had achieved a Neolithic Utopia and then they stopped. And for nearly two thousand years they remained stagnant."

"I don't think you're getting through to me," Julian said. "What's the point?"

The other ignored him. "Now, the Incas were another thing. They too were a Neolithic people to begin with. Ambitious and aggressive, in a couple of centuries they had dominated the Cuzco valley, but it wasn't until about 1440 A.D. that their power exploded. By 1493 they ruled from Quito, Ecuador, to the Rio Maule in Chile. Their art, particularly in metallurgy and textiles, has not been surpassed to this day. Their engineering of roads, bridges, and irrigation projects was superb. They worked copper, tin, bronze, gold, and silver and knew smelting, alloying, casting, inlaying, soldering, riveting, and incrustation. Their medicine too was higher than the level that prevailed in Europe at the time and their diet was superior. They had even taken to the sea and evidently had craft capable of crossing the Pacific, as noted in Hyderthal's *Kon Tiki* experiment. However, the Inca civilization was no stagnant Utopia, Mr. West, but a vital, expanding, healthy society on its way into the future. In many respects it is a pity the Spanish arrived when they did with their superior weapons. It would have been historically interesting to see what the Incas could have accomplished.''

"Your point?" Julian said impatiently. His new drink had arrived and he began on it.

"My point is," Harrison said, "that man cannot afford Utopia. Man is an aggressive, impatient, striving animal and has been since he issued forth from the caves to conquer his world. He cannot afford to hesitate, to speak of coming to a halt. If he does, he stagnates and eventually dies—as the Egyptian culture died, as the Mayan culture died."

Sean O'Callahan and the quiet Ley nodded. "Yes," Sean agreed. "A Utopia dies."

Julian thought that possibly at last they were getting to the point of this meeting.

He said, "This particular Utopia doesn't seem to be dying. It's developing like crazy in all directions."

Harrison shook his head. "No. Not as it should be. Ninety-eight percent of our population is not being utilized. They sit around doing make-work. Our civilization is stagnating, Mr. West."

"Yeah," Ley echoed. "Back in the 1960s and earlier, if somebody had it on the ball, he could fight his way to the top, make his mark on the world. Look at Hitler. Started off as a poor boy and fought his way up to be the most powerful man in the world. And he didn't need any goddamned computers to tell him whether or not he could do it."

Sean laughed lightly. "Not exactly the example I would use," he said.

William Dempsey Harrison brought forth his transceiver and flicked the stud for the time. "I'm afraid I'm going to have to be running along." He looked at Julian. "There's quite a bit more I wanted to discuss with you, but perhaps you've got enough to reflect upon. Can we get together again?"

"Why, of course." In actuality, Julian didn't know exactly where he stood with this man, or how he felt about him. Obviously, the other wasn't satisfied with the status quo. Thus far, Julian West had met only the Leetes, who were. He wouldn't mind knowing a bit more about what was wrong with Utopia.

Harrison stood. "I'll get in touch through Sean, here." He hesitated. "Meanwhile, if you don't mind, I'd appreciate it if you didn't mention this conversation to any of the Leete family."

Chapter Six

The Year 1968

THE SESSION with Harrison, Ley, and O'Callahan hadn't left him feeling very balanced. On his return from the Cub Bar he had gone immediately to bed, only to have one of his worst nightmares ever.

Though all of the war dreams were bad, it was the worst. Certainly it was one of the longest. It invariably started at the same point and ended at the same point, and it always took long minutes to get over.

Captain Julian West returned to Fire Base 2224 in a slick (as the grunts called helicopters) that was large enough to hold six men. It was equipped with sliding doors on both sides. These were open so that the two gunners, who were strapped to either side, could lean out and fire their .30 caliber machine guns if required.

Julian had spent almost two weeks at the hospital in Truj Hoa and then pulled down another week of R & R—rest and relaxation—in Bangkok. Actually, it had been only a minor wound but he was returning with a Bronze Star, a Purple Heart, and, of all things, the Vietnamese Cross of Gallantry; none of which he would bother to mention to his buddies, not particularly wanting to be laughed at.

The chopper swooped into the LZ, the helicopter landing zone for the fire base. The pilot didn't bother to turn off the engine. Julian West took up his duffle bag, waved a brief good bye, and jumped to the ground. The usual cloud of whirling dust, pieces of paper, and dry sticks were being kicked up by the aircraft's blades. He waded hurriedly through the dust as fine as a dark red talcum powder.

Three weeks hadn't much changed Fire Base 2224, although they seemed to have thrown up more entrenchments and strung more wire. He wondered if Charlie was still giving them a hard time. The fire base was located on a hill in the jungle south of Cheo Reo and for the first month or so that the Americans had occupied it, the Viet Cong hadn't been very active in the vicinity. The ambush in which he had been hit had come as a surprise.

There were twenty pieces of artillery and fifteen mortars, the latter of which looked like nothing so much as black stovepipes about three feet high. The artillery crews managed to keep the black guns spotless, in spite of the red dust, by endlessly wiping them with oil rags.

Julian made his way toward his billet. He didn't know if the colonel would be on the hill or not, but he figured on leaving his bag and possibly cleaning up a little before reporting in. The bunkers were little more than big holes in the hillside, covered with logs and heaped high with sandbags. He assumed his billet which he shared with Lieutenant Chenowith, one of his subordinates, was still being retained for him.

He peered down. "Jesus Christ, it's Jule," Turk Chenowith exclaimed, "I thought you got yourself a nice deal back in Saigon. What'd you want to come back here humping around the jungle for?"

"Nice deal? That'll be the day," Julian said, tossing his duffle bag to one side. "I was shafted."

"Here, have a can of beer," Turk offered. He was a small man, the wonder of the company: somehow he managed to be a dandy, even in combat areas. Somehow his uniform was always impossibly neat; somehow he found water with which to shave and wash.

Now he took up a can of beer from an open carton, popped it open and handed it over.

Julian took it gratefully and sat down on one of the empty wooden boxes the bunker boasted in the way of furniture. "What's been happening? Made any new contacts since I've been gone?"

Turk wiped his mouth with the back of his hand. "Pretty bad, but nothing for the last few days. In our company, Buck Dillard's been wasted. Took a handful of rocket frags in his chest. Sergeant Karp and three of his men ran into a whole company of NVAs and had to be dusted off in a Medevac chopper. D Company's had even more casualties than we have. They lost Captain Somerlot."

"Waxed?" Julian asked, pulling at his beer.

The other shook his head. "No. He took three hits in his right leg. They got him back to the base hospital okay, but he was bleeding like a stuck pig from an artery hit up near the groin. He'll never be back; he'll lose the leg. Lucky bastard."

Julian stared at him.

Turk opened another can for himself before he said, "What the hell, I'd trade a leg to get out of 'Nam."

Julian finished his beer. "Is the colonel up at the command post?"

"Yeah. At least he was there half an hour ago. He's sent out D Company to see if they can make contact."

Julian came to his feet. "I better report in. Who's been in charge of the company?"

"I have."

"Any replacement for Buck Dillard yet?"

"No. And none for Sergeant Karp, either. He was the best grunt in my platoon. He was crazy to have stayed in after getting through Korea."

Just as Julian got ready to leave the bunker, a grunt stuck his head down and yelled, "Incoming! We got incoming!"

"Any better place to be than here?" he asked Turk.

"Hell no. I've got enough sandbags on this bunker to stop a direct hit from a 122 millimeter rocket— which, by the way, the Chinese are evidently supplying the NVAs with in this vicinity."

"Great," Julian muttered. He raised his head from the bunker. He could hear the whistle of the rockets. You couldn't see them but you sure could hear them. There was a bright blue flash not so far off and the ground heaved. He threw himself back and down. It had been a close one, all right: he could hear clods of earth that had been thrown high, falling back to the ground, and the smell of smoke was in the air.

There was a small PRC-25 radio in each bunker housing an officer or non-com. It squawked now, then, "Lieutenant Chenowith? Colonel Fry. I'm at the command post. Get over here on the double."

"Yes sir. Colonel. . . ?"

Julian could sense the impatience in the strained voice. "Yes?"

"Captain West has just returned. He's here."

"Oh? Well, send him over instead. You stay where you are. We're short of officers. I don't want to lose both of you."

Julian eyed his lieutenant in disgust. "My pal," he muttered. "Listen to all that stuff going off out there."

Turk put his hand over his heart. "Better you than me, sir."

Julian took up his steel pot and put it on his head. He grabbed up an M-16, and a bandolier of ammo which he slung over his shoulder. He worked a shell into the chamber from the eighteen-round magazine before leaving the shelter of the bunker. It was a light gun, a result of the stock and grip being made of fiberglass, of 5.63 millimeter caliber. It made quite a difference in combat; a man could carry double the ammunition that had been possible with the heavy Garand of the Second World War and Korea, with its .30 caliber.

Crouching under fire, he ran desperately for the command post some two hundred yards up the hill.

Company D had made contact with a thus far undetermined number of Charlie. Air support had been called in and even as Julian entered the jungle with Company B, he could see five jets flying over, going like a flash. In the distance, they peeled off and went in for the kill, firing their machine guns and two rockets each. Bombs as well, judging by the sound of the explosions. And at least one must have dropped a barrel of napalm, he figured as a burst of orange and black erupted over tree level.

The artillery on the fire post was also in action now, the deafening sound a welcome change from the detonations of the 122 millimeter Chinese rockets that had slammed into the base.

Company B marched into the jungle in the usual manner: three columns, right flank, center file, left flank. Julian West and Sergeant Carl Teichert led the center file. Usually they couldn't see the men on the flanks because of the trees, vines, and underbrush. In fact, since the men were spaced approximately thirty feet from each other, they couldn't see many in their own column.

Julian alternated with the sergeant as point man. He carried the M-16, his favorite weapon. Flick the selector on AUTO and press the trigger and you could empty the eighteen-round magazine in something like a second. Of course, that wasn't the usual way you did it, particularly when firing at a definite target. The thing was to press the trigger lightly, a mere flick and then release it, which gave you a burst of three or four rounds.

Sergeant Teichert carried a CAR-15, his own favorite. Behind him Forry Jackson had an M-16 with an over-and-under grenade launcher attached to it. Next came another grunt rifleman and behind him a crew of three men with an M-60 belt-fed machine gun.

The center file was the safest if they ran into an ambush—and in this jungle a hidden Charlie could be as little as ten feet from you without being detected until he started firing. It would most likely be the right or left flank that got it first.

The sergeant, an old combat buddy, had protested Julian's taking the lead, although he usually did.

"Fer Chrissakes, sir, you're the captain. You give the orders. Send us grunts in. We lose you and we don't have no officer."

"I don't like to send a man in where I'm afraid to go myself."

"You just got out of the hospital for doing that, sir."

"That's enough, Sergeant. Let's go. I'll take the first hour of walking point, then you can take it."

"Yes sir."

The sergeant was a good man. Like Sergeant Karp, he was a veteran of Korea, as well as two hitches here in 'Nam.

Now Julian said to Siu Priu, one of the three Vietnamese assigned to the company as interpreters, "You three stick to the center of the column. You're not expendable. I don't know why in the hell Saigon doesn't set up some schools to teach more of you Vietnamese English. We could cooperate better."

"Yis, sor," Siu Priu said.

"That's English?" Sergeant Teichert demanded. "Some interpreter." He didn't like gooks, not even those on the American side, and didn't go to the bother of disguising the fact.

Marking your way through the jungle was slow work, particularly when you knew that Charlie was in the vicinity. They had a nasty habit of sinking Bouncing Bettys into the ground. You stepped on one and the initial charge bounced it up about four or five feet, and then it blew frags in all directions. The irony of it was that they were American-made mines, either captured from the Americans, or bought by the Viet Cong from South Vietnamese who would sometimes sell a part, or all, of their equipment when in need of a wad of Military Payment Certificates, the money of the 'Nam war.

They plowed on through, Julian alternating with the sergeant as point, watching the ground immediately before their feet, darting looks into the trees and brush to either side.

Suddenly, just as they had started up a low hill, the jungle erupted into a Götterdämmerung of sounds. Tracers reached out at them—green tracers, Charlie's tracers. To the right, a RPG rocket-propelled grenade went off. Julian didn't know if it was the enemy's or their own. He was down on one knee, behind a tree. He fired and fired into the jungle.

Teichert went down suddenly some twenty meters ahead, yelling, "Medic! Oh Christ, Medic!"

Julian looked back over his shoulder. There was a lot of firing going on but the only man he could spot was Forry Jackson, calmly launching grenade after grenade in the direction of Charlie.

He dropped his gun and rucksack and, crouching low, ran for his wounded sergeant. Lead and steel were flicking through the leaves of the trees like bees, thudding when they struck the trunks.

He got to Teichert, and dropped down on his knees.

"Get me out of here, Captain," the other wheezed, his face ghost-pale. "I'm hit bad."

Julian could see that he had taken three hits in the stomach. Where the hell was a medic? Teichert was bleeding all over the place. He fumbled for his first aid kit and pressure bandages.

And that was when he took his own hits. It must have been a grenade, although he hadn't heard it.

He stared down at his upper leg, at a purple spot welling larger and larger. He could feel the wound pulsing. An artery: he could bleed to death in minutes.

He started hobbling down the trail, holding his hand over the wound.

Behind him, Sergeant Teichert called weakly, "Don't leave me . . ."

He came to the tree where he had left his gun and rucksack, and sank down, afraid to go further for fear that movement would increase the bleeding.

Not far down the trail he could hear the M-60 chattering. The men had got it set up in short order.

"Medic!" he screamed. "Goddammit, Medic!"

One came hurrying up. He slapped a pressure bandage and a tourniquet on Julian's leg and said, "You're all right."

"Teichert's up the trail. Belly wounds. Hurry, for shit's sake!"

The medic ran. When he came back, he said, "He's dead. If I got to him just a minute sooner . . ."

It was there the dream ended and Julian woke up, sweat-drenched as usual, the memory flooding through him: Teichert bleeding to death while his own comparatively minor wounds occupied the medic's time; deserting his combat buddy, alone on the trail, to save his own skin. . . .

When he had recovered, they gave him a promotion and awarded him the Distinguished Service Cross. The citation read that he had gallantly led his men into combat against serious odds; that when one of his men fell he had gone into enemy fire to rescue him.

That's what the citation said, but he knew better, and he told the psychiatrist so.

The doctor looked at him speculatively. It was their third session. He said, ''You did what you could.''

''No I didn't.''

''If you had remained, you might both have died.''

Julian just shook his head.

''How many times have you been seriously wounded?''

''Three.''

The psychiatrist looked down at the papers on his desk. He took a deep breath and reached for his pen.

''Major, I am recommending that you be discharged and returned to the States.''

Chapter Seven

The Year 2, New Calendar

To waste, to destroy, our natural resources. To skin and exhaust the land instead of using it so as to increase its usefulness, will result in undermining in the days of our children the very prosperity which we ought by right to hand down to them amplified and developed.
　　　　　　　　　　—Theodore Roosevelt

JULIAN HAD BEEN so upset by his Vietnamese nightmare that he had skipped breakfast and taken himself to the Leete apartment down the hall. He found the doctor standing at the window, looking out over the university campus, his face thoughtful. Edith was sitting at the desk, a stylo in hand, making notes.

She looked up at his entrance, smiled and said, "Good morning, Jule."

He crossed to her. "What are you up to? I thought you always made notes into the International Data Banks."

"Oh, I've just been doing some planning for my vacation next year. I've never been to Egypt before."

"Egypt? I never liked the place, particularly the Egyptians. How long do you have?"

"A year. I'm going to help build the pyramid."

He looked at her blankly. "Build the pyramid? What pyramid?"

"Cheops. Archaeology and history students and, well, buffs are going to do a complete replica of the original pyramid of Cheops."

"Cheops! That's the largest of them all!"

"Yes. Exciting, isn't it?" She smiled enthusiastically.

He shook his head in bewilderment. "Well, at least you'll have modern machinery."

"Oh, no. We're going to use all the original methods as a way of figuring out how they accomplished it. Methods and materials."

"But *why*?"

"What better way to study archaeology? We're going to have to figure out, mostly from hieroglyphic inscriptions and so forth, just how the Egyptians quarried, and how they got the stones across the Nile. We'll have to make papyrus boats such as they used. We'll use the same sort of rollers they did. . . ."

"You mean you're going to pull those king-sized

stones by hand? How many of you are in on this crackpot idea?"

"Over ten thousand so far. Mostly students from United America, but a good many from other countries too. It's all the thing among archaeology buffs."

"But it will take years!"

"Of course. And each year some of us will have to drop away, but others will take their place. When it's all finished, it will be a museum, and for tourists to see, and so forth. It will look exactly the way the original did when it was first completed, and it will be close enough to the original that one will be able to walk between them to compare."

"Look," he said almost desperately, "why in the hell don't you start on something easier? Something like rebuilding the Acropolis in Athens, complete with the Parthenon?"

"Oh, some European students are doing that."

"Then why not start with one of the smaller pyramids, something not quite so ambitious? Down in Yucatan, maybe. One of the Mayan pyramids."

"Oh, the Mexicans and other Meso-American specialists are doing that. I'm an Egyptologist, with a concentration in the first five dynasties."

"I thought you were a farmer."

"I am. That's my work. But Egyptian archaeology and anthropology is one of my hobbies."

He shook his head and went over to stand next to Doctor Leete. The doctor still had somewhat of a shiner from his fracas of the day before.

Julian asked, "Have you figured out why those fellows jumped you?"

Leete looked at him and frowned. "I'm not sure. If you don't mind, Julian, I'd rather not talk about it, at least until I'm more certain of my facts. The whole thing is quite unprecedented."

"As you wish. I don't want to pry."

"How go the studies?"

"I'm still concentrating on learning Interlingua, but yesterday I got a resume of scientific and technological breakthroughs that have occurred since I went into stasis. I've got quite a few questions I'd like to ask you."

"Ah? Fire away. That's my assignment."

Julian gestured at the view out over the campus. "I'm continually amazed by the abundance; how you ever got to the point, in a third of a century, where you produce so much more than we used to, is a complete mystery to me."

The doctor seemed amused. "We don't produce more than you used to. We produce *less*, I'm sure."

Julian looked at him as though he were joking. "That's ridiculous. Everyone lives on a scale that only the wealthy could afford in 1970."

Leete chuckled, then gestured that they should take seats. "It's not how much you produce but what you produce and how you distribute it. You measured your product in 1970 in dollars. Just how great was your yearly production?"

"Gross National Product was approximately a trillion dollars."

The doctor thought about that. "In actuality, that takes a bit of qualification. The method of calculating that Gross National Product had its weak points."

"How do you mean? It was simply the combined

products and services of the whole population.''

The doctor pursed his lips. ''Well, let's take one example. The United States had long been proud of its per capita production as compared to that of other advanced countries, say, Sweden, or the Soviet Union. Let us say we have an American surgeon who makes twenty-five thousand dollars a year. That amount is added to the supposed total of the Gross National Product. In Sweden, his equal is paid but ten thousand dollars a year, since medicine is socialized there. Thus, in calculating Sweden's Gross National Product, the doctor's contribution is but ten thousand dollars. Over in Leningrad, a Soviet surgeon, the exact equal in ability to his American and Swedish colleagues, is paid but five thousand dollars a year, working for the state. In calculating Russian GNP, that sum is part of the total.

''And that isn't the end. The following year, the American decides to get on the gravy train, as the expression goes, and moves to New York where he doubles his fees and makes fifty thousand dollars a year. So he now contributes ten times as much to the GNP as does his Soviet equal.''

Julian had to laugh.

''Nor is that all,'' the doctor went on. ''Let us leave services and take definite products. The Japanese of your time were turning out compact automobiles that were built to last. Some of them utilized the Wankel rotary engine, which gave good mileage and emitted very little in the way of pollution. American cars selling for the same amount, on the contrary, were built with planned obsolescence in mind. Detroit wanted the customer to desire a new car approximately every three years. Suppose that each of these cars cost three thousand dollars. The Japanese car gave double or more the mileage and lasted at least twice as long. Is it, then, accurate to add to the GNP of both the United States and Japan the amount of three thousand dollars?"

"I see what you mean," Julian said. "GNP can be a somewhat elastic term. But what's this got to do with your producing less than we used to? On the face of it——"

"Once again," the doctor interrupted, "it's a matter of what you produce and how you distribute it. For instance, we no longer produce weapons of destruction. What was your yearly bill for war, preparation for war, and paying off past wars?"

"I think it was pushing a hundred billion a year," Julian said. "We even had widows on the pension lists who went back to the Civil War and the Indian Wars."

"That took a considerable portion of the product of your trillion dollar economy. We have no military today. Also, in your day you had a top-heavy bureaucracy of some ten million persons, very few of whom produced anything worthwhile for the nation. Their labors were largely wasted."

"You still have government workers."

"Yes, but now they are part of the production process and are necessary. And most certainly they are fewer in number. But most important, your socioeconomic system was one of waste: your automobiles with power steering, power windows, air conditioning, engines which could drive them over one hundred twenty miles an hour but got only seven to ten miles to the gallon. The Japanese cars I mentioned before got up to thirty. And while it was possible to produce cars that could have lasted half a century, few American cars lasted ten years. Today, we build our cars to last as long as possible.

"But that's only the beginning. In your grandfather's day, when he bought a watch he expected it to last the rest of his life. Indeed, he often willed it to his son. By your time, they were turning out watches so poorly made that when one stopped, the owner simply threw it away and bought a new one. It was cheaper than having it repaired, or even cleaned. Today, once again, we manufacture watches that will last as long as possible—when we use watches at all; usually we dial the time on our transceivers. I remember, when I was a boy, cigarette lighters that were meant to be thrown away when they had used up their fuel, rather than refilled. Many of the ballpoint pens were the same—non-refillable. And planned obsolescence didn't apply only to cars. Kitchen appliances, light bulbs, tires, batteries, furniture—just about all products. You used throwaway bottles and so-called tin cans by the billions each year."

"Wait a minute," Julian said. "What do you do with tin cans today?"

"Actually, we use them very infrequently," the other told him. "For instance, we prefer our food fresh. When we do use cans the metal is recycled. Mainly, we use plastic containers and the plastic too can be recycled."

Julian said, "It seems to me that you can carry that recycling bit to an extreme. Suppose you go on a picnic way out in the boondocks somewhere and you take along a a dozen bottles or cans of beer. After you're finished, do you have to carry them all the way back home to be thrown into the disposal chute and recycled?''

The doctor smiled. ''Hardly. We have a special type of plastic for such use. In two or three days, exposure to either sun or rain will cause it to melt away into the ground. It is not harmful to soil.''

''Isn't that waste?''

Leete nodded agreement. ''Yes. But we are not fanatical. Also, it is not as though we were throwing away cans made of steel or aluminum. The plastic is made from wood and other things that grow and hence are replaceable.''

''You must use up a good many trees, if you manufacture as much plastic as all that.''

''There have been advances in forestry since your time, Julian. We now have trees that grow to maturity in one year. And, with nuclear fision and solar power, it is practical to desalinate ocean water and pump it into such areas as the Sahara and the Arabian and Gobi deserts. They are rapidly being reforestrated. We use wood and other agricultural products wherever we can, rather than metals and such irreplaceable natural resources. We husband such things for future generations. Such metals as we do utilize are recycled over and over again.''

The doctor paused. ''Another example of waste in your time was your houses. In Europe today there are houses many hundreds of years old that are still lived in. Back at the time of the American Revolution, there were homes built that are still in existence. But in your day? A homeowner with a thirty-year mortgage could expect the house to have deteriorated before he finished paying for it. So bad was the workmanship and the materials that many had become hovels or shacks before ten years were up. Today, as in the long-ago past, we build houses that will last for centuries."

"I suppose you're right there," Julian begrudged him. "We constructed millions of buildings each year and tore down almost an equal number—not just houses, but every other type of building as well."

"Another great waste of your time," Leete went one, "was power. You were going through your fossil fuels such as petroleum, coal, and natural gas as though there was an unlimited supply. For example, everyone who could afford it air-conditioned not only their homes, their offices, their stores and public buildings, but their cars as well."

"You mean to tell me that you no longer use air-conditioning?"

"Sometimes, but not the to the extent you did. You see, most of us have come to believe that man's body was designed for the temperatures nature provides. It did your health little good to go back and forth from the heat outside to air-conditioned interiors. How many colds and other respiratory diseases resulted from the practice, we'll never know. You also drastically overheated your buildings in the winter months. Today, we still heat our houses, of course, but we are more inclined to wear heavier clothing, warm underwear and sweaters, rather than swelter in summer temperatures in December. Why, those who could afford it even heated their swimming pools.

Can you imagine the amount of power that consumed?"

"That's one of the things I meant to ask you about," Julian said. "When I went into stasis, we were beginning to face a power shortage. How did you lick that? Though, from what you say, you now have unlimited power from nuclear fision."

"It's not as simple as all that," Leete told him. "Unlimited power through nuclear fision could bring with it unlimited heat, which would be bound to get us into all sorts of trouble. So although we utilize it to some degree, we also call upon other sources, particularly renewable energy sources, so that we can live on the earth's energy income, rather than its capital. We now utilize much more wind and water power—even the tides. We tap the heat of the interior of the planet. But most of all we are calling upon solar power, the vast energy pouring down on us from the sun. It produces some fifty thousand times as much energy as man's current rate of consumption."

Julian, as usual, was lost. He said, "You and Edith have mentioned solar power several times and although they were working on it even earlier than 1960, I never did quite understand it. You know, that was true about just almost everybody in my day. We accepted things but didn't have the vaguest idea of how they worked. For instance, I don't know what radio is, not really. It goes in here and it comes out there, but I haven't the slightest idea of just what happens. I was an average citizen, with an average citizen's knowledge of the gadgets we had; I haven't the vaguest idea what makes a refrigerator cold. But back to solar power. . . .I think there were some two hundred houses completely, or at least mostly, powered by solar sources, even in my time."

Leete nodded. "The solar battery was developed by the Bell Telephone Laboratories in 1954. It's been improved considerably since then. The early batteries were a flat sandwich of n-type and p-type semi-conductors. Sunlight striking the plate would knock some electrons out of place. The transfer was connected, as in the ordinary-type battery, in an electrical circuit. The freed electrons move toward the positive pole and holes move toward the negative pole, thus constituting a current. Those early solar batteries developed electric potentials of up to half a volt and up to nine watts of power from each square foot exposed to the sun. Not very much, perhaps, but its advantage was that it had no liquids, no corrosive chemicals, no moving parts. Electricity continued to be generated indefinitely, so long as the sun shined."

"You've already lost me," Julian said. "I'm afraid I'm no science student."

"It is a bit technical," the doctor agreed. "The amount of energy falling upon one acre of a sunny area of the earth is 9.4 million kilowatt-hours per year. Square mile upon square mile have been covered with solar batteries in places such as parts of the Sahara not suited for reforestation, in Death Valley, in the deserts of what was once Utah and other parts of the West. The Chinese have emplaced them in areas of the Gobi and the Russians in desert areas of Siberia. The Arabs have a source of power as great as that of their oil of the mid-twentieth century, in the broiling sun of the Arabian peninsula. In short, Julian, in solar power we have a source of energy that will undoubtedly last as long as the human race endures.''

''What's wrong with nuclear atomic reactors? You have unlimited power from hydrogen taken from the oceans. They were the thing when I went into stasis.''

''Radioactive wastes are more carefully handled now, but there is still danger. The United States Atomic Energy Commission, the official custodian of the deadly byproducts of the nuclear age, took calculated risks which, looking backward, have horrified us. For instance, back in the early nineteen seventies more than a half million gallons of deadly radioactive liquid leaked from huge storage tanks at the AEC's Hanford facility, near Richmond, Washington.

''No, we are leery about nuclear power and I have no doubt that they will phase it out as our power resources from solar energy continue to grow. Perhaps future generations will revive its use again, when science has learned more about handling it.''

Edith Leete put down her stylo, got up from the desk, and took a chair nearer to them. ''I can't concentrate with you two jabbering away,'' she said. ''I thought you were talking about waste under the old system. You hardly touched on some of the major ways there were to throw away valuable products.''

Julian looked at her. ''Such as?''

''Take something like clothing. In your day, there were thousands of clothing manufacturers in this country alone. They would design, say, a woman's dress, keeping their fingers crossed that the potential customer would go for the lower hem or higher hem, the lower waist or the higher waist, or this, that, or the other thing in the way of style. The shopper had tens of thousands of stores to choose from, ranging from tiny one-room affairs to department stores covering acres of land. There were mail-order houses which put out catalogues as large as the phone book of a considerable city. No woman could begin to examine all the varieties of dresses manufactured to part her from her dollars.''

Julian took in the coverall-type garment she wore, which was almost identical to that he and the doctor were garbed in.

He said, an edge of sarcasm to his voice, ''In my day, people, and women in particular, dressed for attractiveness. Now everybody wears the same thing. I'm not so sure I don't prefer the old days.''

The doctor laughed, but let his daughter carry the ball.

She smiled, looking down at her outfit. ''These aren't the only clothes we wear. They just happen to be the uniform, more or less, of the university. They're practical, comfortable, suitable for anything from laboratory work to most sports. But I wouldn't expect to go to a party, or dancing, or skiing . . .'' she grinned at him ''. . . or swimming in these dungarees.''

''Okay,'' Julian acknowledged. ''But then what's the difference between 1970 and the Year 2, New Calendar?''

''To get back to our woman buying a dress. She could choose among tens of thousands of dresses and so forth. So big was the choice that if she went shopping, she couldn't possibly check out everything. Besides that, she had a choice of quality, superior and inferior textiles, cheaper and more expensive designs. In our system there is still a choice, but there are only a few hundred different designs. And all textiles are the best possible; there are no inferior materials."

"But isn't it monotonous?" Julian argued.

Edith laughed. "A few hundred basic dresses is no small matter. Three hundred different types of skirts, three hundred different types of blouses, three hundred sweaters, three hundred belts, three hundred shoes and sandals. Work that out mathematically and you can see that you have literally hundreds of thousands of potential costumes. But if you are still unhappy, you can buy material and design your own clothing. A good many women do, and more men are drifting into it too. Textile design and making your own clothing are growing hobbies these days. The big thing is that we don't produce and then destroy literally millions of articles of clothing each year simply because they have gone out of fashion. For all practical purposes, styles and fashions as such have disappeared. Our clothing is made for comfort, to be warm or cool as the season dictates, and to be attractive without being garish or ridiculous. We wouldn't dream of wearing anything as silly as a girdle, nor a tie on a man."

"As you say," Julian sighed. "I'll admit we had some far-out fads in our day. You should have seen some of the hats."

Doctor Leete had been silent while his daughter sounded off on the subject of style. He said, "It seems to me that when I was a boy in my teens, one of the greatest wastes was the lack of planning of production. Under capitalism, capital flowed to where profit was greatest. Suppose, for instance, artichokes became a food fad. Prices would go up. Thousands of farmers would immediately put in crops of artichokes. They would overflow the market. Prices would break. Then tons upon tons of artichokes would become surplus and rot in the fields since it wouldn't be worth harvesting them.

"Or take something like toys. Do you remember the Davy Crockett fad? I barely do. Suddenly Davy Crockett coonskins hats, Davy Crockett frontiersman shirts, Davy Crockett moccasins were a must for every child. Hundreds of manufacturers leaped in to profit in the market. Then, overnight, the youngsters tired of Davy Crockett and found a new fad, leaving literally millions of coonskin hats and moccasins to mold in warehouses or be destroyed. As far as a reasonable socioeconomic system was concerned, it was anarchy."

Edith yawned mightily and said, "I'm getting bored with all this talk. If poor Julian hasn't already become convinced that the socioeconomic system under which he lived was a madhouse compared to today, he never will. Jule, how would you like to take a drive out to our home? I have some things I have to pick up."

He looked at her quizzically. "Your home? Isn't this your home?"

"Oh, good heavens, Jule. This is a university city. We're just in residence here while Father continues his research on your case and while I study various projects of mine. Mother is taking a few courses too."

"Let's go," Julian said.

Chapter Eight

The Year 2, New Calendar

Animal's lives utterly depend upon green plants. Plants alone give us our food; they alone renew and refresh the air, they alone recycle organic wastes, and they alone store sunlight for our use. Plants must have ground space on which to grow. Buildings and roads are using it up at ever-faster speed. . . . Therefore, those of us who build and pave are helping to plunge the planet into disaster. Obviously, then, since we can't change the facts of life, we've got to change the way we pave and build. Buildings and roads below the living green surface of the land can restore ground space to life again.

—Malcolm B. Wells, Architect

EDITH AND JULIAN TOOK the elevator to the car pool in the basement of the high-rise apartment building in which they lived.

He said, "This pyramid project you're interested in simply floors me. I just don't get the why of it."

She looked amused. "When Father told you that only two percent of the population was needed in industry to produce an abundance for all, did you come to the conclusion that the remaining ninety-eight percent spent their time sitting before the Tri-Di television, guzzling beer and pushing pleasure buttons?"

"Pleasure buttons?"

She laughed. "It's a branch of medical science that was experimented with for a time and then definitely dropped. I believe the experiments started with rats and monkeys back before you went into stasis. It was possible, electronically, to stimulate the areas of the brain relating to pleasure. By activating a button, the animal would experience the height of pleasure momentarily. Push the button again and the pleasure returned again, and over and over. Nothing else made any difference to them. Food, drink, even sex meant nothing. They would remain, pressing the button until they fell over from exhaustion, starvation, or dehydration."

"Good God!" Julian exclaimed. "You mean that brain specialists can do that to humans as well?"

She nodded. "Can, but don't. Not all the roads opened up by science are followed, Julian. So far as pleasure is concerned, we like to find it ourselves—normally. One of the ways is to create beauty. Much of the beauty in the world, created in the past, has been lost to us. We are attempting to recreate that which we can. For instance, did you know that of the Seven Wonders of the Ancient World, only the ruins of the

Pyramid of Cheops is still in existence? All of the others we are attempting to rebuild: the Colossus of Rhodes, the Hanging Gardens of Babylon, the Mausoleum at Halicarnassus, the Artemision at Ephesus, the Olympian Zeus statue originally by Phidias, the Pharos lighthouse.''

He simply stared at her in open-mouthed wonder.

The elevator had reached the car pool. Edith spoke into a screen, ordering a two-seater. Within moments it sped up to where they stood.

''I'll drive,'' she said. ''I know all the coordinates.''

They got in and she deftly dialed their destination.

''Where are we going?'' he asked as the automated car took off. He still wasn't used to seeing the driver with hands not on the wheel.

''Our semi-permanent home is in what you used to call Maryland. A small town called Hopewell.''

''Semi-permanent?'' he repeated. ''Then you don't own it?''

The car blended into the underground traffic, moving into the inner and fastest line.

She shook her head. ''Nobody owns their homes now, Jule. It doesn't make sense.''

''In my time, most of us—those who could afford to own them—took pride in our homes.''

''We take pride in them too as long as we remain in residence. That is, we beautify them, keep them as comfortable and attractive as we can. But we don't tie ourselves down to one house, as a rule. Oh, some people do. Some live in the same dwelling all their lives. Certainly, there is no one to say them nay. But usually we rent our homes until some reason comes up that makes it practical to move."

"Such as?"

"Well, look. Here you are a single man. It would seem unlikely that you would want a large house. Although housework is almost completely automated, there are still things that must be done. You rent a smallish house, or an apartment, in an area that is desirable to you, say in the mountains. Very well, after a time you meet a girl and form a permanent or semi-permanent arrangement with her. Obviously, a somewhat larger house is called for. Lo and behold, the following year she has a baby. A larger house is called for. Besides that, you're getting tired of the mountains and move down to Florida for the beach and the fishing. It turns out she loves children and since you're both genetically ideal, you are given the go-ahead to have another child. You decide you could use another room. So it goes for a few years and the first baby grows up and goes off on his own. Shortly the other child matures and leaves as well. There are just two of you now. You decide you've had enough of Florida anyway, and move down to one of the picturesque old Spanish Colonial towns in what was called Mexico before it was amalgamated into United America. By this time, your girlfriend is getting sick and tired of you and leaves. You are now single again, and a one-person house is in order. Doesn't it make sense?"

"I suppose so," he said. "Actually, in my time, too, we had a lot of people who were continually moving. But look, to get back to rebuilding the pyramid and all the Seven Wonders. If they're destroyed, how can you recreate them?"

"It's a problem, all right. Scholars are digging up every bit of information they can find. There are illustrations, some written descriptions. For instance, the lighthouse at Pharos was built back in Ptolemy's day, before Christ, but it lasted until the 14th Century A.D. Many times it was depicted on pottery, on Egyptian tomb walls, on papyrus. We've got a pretty good idea of what the lighthouse looked like, and the Colossus of Rhodes which, by the way, didn't straddle the harbor as it is sometimes illustrated. We're having more trouble, actually, with the Roman Forum, which wasn't one of the Seven Wonders, but we're going to redo it anyway."

"The Roman Forum! It must have covered several square miles, including the Colosseum. I've seen it."

"Yes, of course. You see, it lasted for well over a thousand years. Now, do we reconstruct it as it was in the days of Lars Porsenna and the Etruscan reges, or as it looked during the time of Caesar and Augustus? In Nero's day, or that of Marcus Aurelius when it was probably at the height of its beauty?"

"Next you'll be telling me you've got a project for damming up the Mississippi River so it'll flow backward over the Rocky Mountains," he protested.

She just smiled. The car began to edge over to the slower lanes. Finally, it darted off onto a smaller road and shortly began to ascend a ramp. A red light flickered on the dash and Edith took over the controls. They emerged into the countryside. "You mean we're here already?" Julian asked.

"We were doing about three hundred kilometers," Edith said. "But we're not quite there yet. However, this part of Maryland is so beautiful I thought you'd probably rather see the countryside than continue any longer in the underground. Frankly, I hate the darn things. It's as though you're in suspended animation. But, of course, if speed is the thing, they give it to you."

"Three hundred kilometers? That's about one hundred eighty miles an hour isn't it?"

"Something like that. It's been so long since I've converted miles to kilometers that I'd have to think about it. Anyway, at that speed, with no stops, no hills, no turns, you can cross the whole country in a little more than ten hours."

He had only twice before driven through the countryside since he had been brought out of hibernation. Once again it took him back to his youth, when his parents or some other relative had sometimes driven him through upper New England in the autumn.

The road was not even paved and the traffic so slight that he felt half-inclined to wave at another car when they passed. He estimated that at least nine-tenths of the traffic of this day was underground. He had already had it explained to him and he supposed it made sense. Unless you were out for some reason such as picnicking, fishing, or just a drive through the countryside, you took to the ultra-highways below ground and got to your destination in a fraction of the time. This road was more suited to a stately forty miles an hour, rather than one hundred eighty.

It was a beautiful day. After the ultra-efficiency high-rise building at the university city, the drive in the country was relaxing. From time to time they would pass a farm house, invariably so put together as to resemble a Hollywood set. Once or twice there were people on the porch or in the yard. Someone waved and Edith and Julian both waved back.

He said, "I thought you didn't have small farms any more."

"We don't. Except for people who make it their hobby."

"You mean none of these places puts in crops?"

"Some do. I've been considering taking a place like one of these after I've retired, or been bumped from my job. They grow their own things, receive pleasure from raising, canning, and drying their own products. Largely, they're older people who remember and liked the old way of life. But some are younger folk who have simply taken it up as a hobby."

"I thought almost everybody lived in high-rise apartment buildings like those at University City."

"Oh, no, very few do. It's a rather sterile way of life, really. The advantage of it in an institution as large as Julian West University City is that it enables a very large number of students to be in a comparatively small area. If they were spread out in individual homes the school area would have to cover several square miles of land and you'd waste all sorts of time getting from one place to another. Well, here we are."

Julian looked about him. "I thought you lived in a town. Hopewell, or whatever you call it."

"This is Hopewell."

"Are you joking?" He looked out over the rolling hills with their numerous trees and other vegetation. But then, to his surprise, he could make out an occasional glint, as of sun on a window, and realized that a good deal of the vegetation was too neat to be simply virgin countryside such as they had been driving through for the past half hour.

Edith, really amused now, turned down a narrow side road, went around a hill, and drove into a small garage.

"Home again," she said, getting out.

He followed her, not having the vaguest idea what was to come. They emerged into a patio, sunk perhaps some twenty feet beneath ground level. Looking up, he could see trees, bushes, flowers, and grass, on what could only be called the roof of the building. Various rooms opened off the patio, all many-windowed in order to take advantage of the sunlight.

Edith led the way. "This is the living room."

It was a large room, possibly twice the size of that in the Leete apartment. The far side consisted mainly of a window under a cantilever, which was also covered with vegetation. Julian looked out over the wooded valley. If there were other houses of this type in the vicinity, he couldn't see them.

With mounting amazement, he took in the furniture, the art work. It was a comfortable, well-lived-in room. He asked, "Is this whole building underground?"

Edith went over to the auto-bar. "Beer? I'm thirsty from our drive. Yes, all the houses in Hopewell are underground. In fact, so are most of the houses in United America. We leave the surface for plant life, for wild animal life. For nature in general."

He flopped down in one of the chairs, looking as bewildered as he felt.

She laughed again, without ridicule, and handed him a glass of beer.

But then the small frown he loved so much brought two light wrinkles to her forehead. "Surely you must have had *some* underground buildings back in the middle of the last century."

"We might have had a few—parking lots and so forth. But as far as homes are concerned, offhand all I can remember are some caves in Southern Spain that the gypsies used to live in. Come to think of it, they were amazingly comfortable. They held flamenco dances in them for the tourists."

"I think Father still has an old brochure by Malcolm B. Wells. I suppose you've heard of him?"

"I don't think so."

"It's possible he's still alive. I guess he was pushing fifty when you went into stasis. He was one of the most progressive architects of your time. Now let me see. . . ." She went over to one of the bookcases and began searching. "Father keeps quite a few old books. He likes to mark them up with notes."

"I thought you had to do all of your reading on the Library Booster Screen."

"Oh, no. Any book in the data banks can be printed up at a very low credit charge and delivered to you. Here we are."

She reached up and selected a rather well-worn brochure, which she handed to him.

"Read this while I activate the house and get a few things done."

"Activate the house?"

"We turn it off when no one is in residence. And we'll be wanting to eat and so forth. Besides, it's a little musty; no one has been here for several months. We've all been caught up in your revival and your first few weeks in this century."

Julian took a deep slug of his beer and began to read.

UNDERGROUND ARCHITECTURE

I can just picture some smelly old bastard, club in hand, the conventional caveman of the comic strips, a prototype Fred Flintstone, surprised at seeing a cave for the first time in his life. It must not have been very many minutes later that the idea of underground architecture was born.

That was perhaps a million years ago, long before modern man, as we know him, evolved. Since that time, of course, man has not exactly been standing still. Not only has he invented war and bigotry (and the religions to excuse them), and learned how to lay continents bare and to overbreed himself, but he has also invented or discovered many, many kinds of shelter other than the cave. Still, architecture—really great architecture—remains, as it began, an earth art; an expression, fashioned in the earth's own materials, of the particular culture in which the man-architect lives. And despite great advances in the techniques of building above ground, man has never completely abandoned underground construction. Fossilized remains from every age, from every continent, prove that man has continued to avail himself of this most ancient of architectures.

Now, though, suddenly, for the first time, in this Twentieth Century, in the face of unchecked population growth, all earth-life faces the prospect of extinction because of man's too rapid successes. He has at last begun to crowd himself from the surface of the planet. But now, too, for the first time, he has both the awareness and the ability *needed to undo some of the earth-damage he has done. Faced with the problems of air and water pollution, water shortages, desperate overcrowding, a disappearing countryside, exhausted soils, and vast famines, man is forced to reappraise many long unquestioned ideas about his relation to the life-giving earth.*

Out of this reappraisal whole new professions are evolving. Today, the growing importance of city planning, demography, soil, water, and wildlife conservation, and the overall science of ecology attest to man's new awareness of the land crisis and his disappearing natural heritage.

Underground architecture for the purpose of conservation *is but one expression of this new land ethic. Buildings already planned for construction in many parts of the United States will use the new practice of re-establishing balanced, natural-type soils above a man-made structure. Then, plant materials selected for both natural beauty and appropriateness to their region will be established on the roofs of the structures so that in the shortest possible number of years, thriving little biotic communities requiring no human maintenance will start to reappear. Future forests.*

Underground architecture, though but one of many far-reaching conservation practices, promises measurable relief in many areas. In the Cherry Hill (Greater Philadelphia) area, for instance, a forty-five-inch annual rainfall amounts to over one million gallons of rainfall per acre each year. Obviously, then, for each acre made impervious by conventional construction (blacktop and roofing materials), over one million gallons of life-giving rain water are wasted each year, sent coursing down streams never intended to accommodate such surges, eroding banks, destroying plants and animal habitats, and finally carrying to the ocean rich topsoils, mineral nutrients, and bacteria that were built up on the land during those long centuries before modern man learned to pave. Underground architecture can prevent such damage by keeping its paved surfaces hidden from the rain. With a young forest to catch it, most of the rainfall on such structures will be held by the foliage and the deep humus layers, some of the water to be used by the plants and animals on the site, and the rest piped directly to the underground reserves now being robbed by conventional construction practices. But not all underground structures need have forests above them. In the West, where drier conditions prevail, hardy natural grasses and wildflowers can adorn such buildings just as they once adorned the prairies themselves. Parks, farms, meadows, and recreational areas can be established above these new buildings. A shopping center designed for the Philadelphia area, for instance, will have an 18-hole golf course above its skylighted stores and parking lots.

Further, underground architecture offers us many immediate, practical advantages. Because of the earth's rather constant fifty-five-degree underground temperature (measurable in caves throughout the world), very little heating and even less air conditioning will be required in such buildings. This, plus almost no need for outside maintenance, snow removal, or lawn sprinklers, add up to considerable savings. In addition such intangibles as isolation from both outside noises and atmospheric radioactivity offer further incentives to build this way. The prospect that we may once more find the great green out-of-doors at our doorsteps makes hoped-for increases in leisure time seem even more appealing.

But the words "underground architecture" often tend to repel the people who hear them. Having been exposed too many times to the depressing look of our subways and highway tunnels, or to leaky basements and cold, damp caves, people tend to view the real advantages of this new architecture with great skepticism. Most people will agree that such land-wasters as parking lots could go below ground. And many will even concede that some of our freeways, shopping centers—even our factories and offices— belong there too (in addition to railroad yards, refineries, and museums). But the thought of living underground in a windowless, artificial environment is to them the ultimate perversion of man's role on earth.

Man, they say, was meant to live in the sun and air, to be involved in the seasons, to know night and day. Fortunately, most advocates of this new architecture heartily agree.

When architects propose windowless, wholly underground buildings, they are not *planning housing.*

Wonderful underground houses have been designed that always open onto sunny, sunken courtyards or project from the sides of hills in order that their rooms can be adequately day-lighted. Such underground buildings will be perfectly dry, and by natural methods will tend to keep the humidity level in the healthful forty to fifty percent range.

Whether or not underground architecture will ever be applied to the downtown areas of our large cities, the fact remains that it has definite application everywhere else. It offers hope that the great, blighted areas around our cities and along our highways may someday become green and beautiful again.

But underground architecture is no cure-all. It is only one way—one legitimate way—of bowing to the great life cycle we're so quickly destroying. Though it has been endorsed by many ecologists and landscape architects, the idea has drawn fire from some who misunderstand it, who fear that it will result in a kind of non-architecture. Regardless, the idea is gaining in popularity each day as more and more people begin to wonder about the blight they see all around them.

Until now, man has always gone underground only for selfish reasons—security, bomb-proofing, or the novelty of dialing his own lighting and "weather" effects. If he continues to build for such reasons he may well create underground structures as ugly and as destructive as those above ground, but if he can find a new respect for the miracle of life—for all of the myraid life forms to which he is related–he may produce an architecture that his descendants will treasure. . . .

Edith returned when he was barely halfway through, but took a chair and remained silent, sipping her beer.

He looked up finally and gestured with the pamphlet. "I don't know. I suppose it makes sense. It just comes as a surprise. How many houses are there like this in Hopewell?"

"Several hundred, I would imagine."

"But where are your stores, your community buildings, your car pool? Or bars, restaurants? And don't you have any sports facilities in a town this big? Swimming pool, tennis courts?"

"They're all underground too, built into the hillsides, sunk below the surface. To the extent possible, we try to avoid any view of man's work. This is the manner in which most people live in America now. In small communities, in areas of beauty, but where modern agriculture isn't very practical. Oh, we have fruit orchards here and there, and the machines come out at night and tend them and harvest them in season; but basically this is residential area."

He shook his head. "I'll have another drink. A stiffer one this time," he said, coming to his feet.

Chapter Nine

The Year 2, New Calendar

It is manifest that a doubling of the world's population in a generation has monstrously distorted traditional patterns. It is manifest that technology is at the bottom of it, specifically modern medicine. All Humanity is affected. . . . The goal of the birth control movement is a balanced society where man and his environment are in reasonable equilibrium, where children are wanted and cared for . . . if a given society desires . . . modern medicine and a low death rate, it must limit its birth rate.

—Stuart Chase,
The Most Probable World

EDITH SHOWED HIM the house in detail and Julian was properly impressed.

He asked, "Down here, away from the elements, how long would you expect a house like this to last?"

111

The question had evidently never occurred to her. "Why, I would think forever, given no serious earthquakes—or something unlikely such as being hit by a good-sized meteor. And always assuming, of course, that social change doesn't bring us to a new politico-economic system that involves the stupidity of wars."

"Knock on wood," her guest muttered.

She said, "You know, in my archaeological studies the other day I was reading about some excavations in Mesopotamia, near Ur. They found a tomb constructed and furnished like a house. Everything was still perfect; in that dry climate not a thing had deteriorated. The walls were made of adobe brick, and so were the floors. The floors had been treated with ox blood and milk, evidently over and over again, so that they were as hard as linoleum, and they had retained their beautiful deep red sheen down through the thousands of years. It seems that underground houses, made with natural materials, can last forever."

"Natural materials?"

"Actually, building materials have come a long way in the past third of a century. Beginning with spin-offs from the space program experiments, our scientists and technicians took off in all directions. For instance, the glass in this house is shatterproof, bullet-proof, and all but indestructible. I'm not up on the subject, but you can investigate it when we get back to the university, if you wish. Let's eat, Jule. I'm starved."

They went into the dining room. Julian said, "You name it. I have yet to have a dish in this era that wasn't delicious."

"How about a mixed grill of liver, kidney, and heart?"

"Sounds good."

Edith dialed and while they waited she said, "Now, cooking is something I know a little about, since mother is such a buff. It's become a fine art. In the past, almost everyone had food prejudices, often inherited from their parents since most cooking was done in the home. 'I'm a meat and potatoes man,' was a proud boast, when it should have been something to be ashamed of. There was precious little variety in most restaurant menus. From coast to coast you would find practically identical fare, and there was a sandwich stand on just about every corner. Now we teach the young people to be gourmets from earliest childhood."

Julian laughed ruefully. "I too have my food prejudices. I could never stand either spinach or squash."

The center of the table dropped, to return with their meal. Edith had ordered salad, vegetables, and a bottle of claret to go with the grill.

He shook his head. "I can't get used to the idea of this meat being factory raised."

"It makes sense," she said. "Raising beef, pork, even chickens in the old manner was terribly inefficient, and practically impossible to automate very much. Take a country like India. In your day, they had hundreds of millions of cows. Can you imagine how much food had to go into each of them each year? And most of the Indians wouldn't even eat beef for religious reasons. Humans starved, while cattle ate half the agricultural products of the country."

Julian said, "And now it's all raised in what

113

amounts to oversized test tubes, in which the necessary nutrients are piped in to continue the life and growth of the various meats. But you still have to have agricultural products to nourish this living—but not really living—flesh.''

"Yes, but much less than when we raised the whole animal. In the factory vats, where the meat grows, there are no bones, no skin, no waste at all. We grow only the parts of the animal we wish to use. Sir, this is a grim subject to discuss while eating.''

Julian agreed. ''All right. Here's something else I wanted to ask you about. When you were kidding me about renting houses rather than owning them, you mentioned the fact that first we had a baby, and then since my—my girl and I were genetically ideal we were given permission to have a second child. That floors me. You mean you have to be genetically checked out before you can have children these days? We wouldn't have stood for that in my time.''

"I worded that poorly,'' she admitted. ''There is no *law* involving such things, but there have been considerable advances in genetics in the past quarter of a century. As a consequence, from earliest youth we are taught how important it is not to have children by someone whose genes are such that the child might be affected adversely. So it is that practically any couple considering children will have themselves throughly checked out.''

"Even if a couple were told that a child of theirs would be a Mongolian idiot, they could go ahead if they wished?''

"Yes. You can see how extremely unlikely that would be, but there is no law against it. We've eliminated laws having to do with individual actions that don't harm anyone else. If you want to read pornography you can do so until your eyes drop out. If you want to take dope until you're so far around the bend that you have to be hospitalized, go ahead—just so long as you don't harm someone else. If you're a homosexual, have the time of your life—but make sure your partner is a consenting adult."

"So that genetic thing is voluntary."

"That's right."

Julian took another sip of his wine. "What's happened to the population explosion? What's the population now? What is it in India, for heaven's sake?"

She looked at him in surprise. "You continually set me back with your lack of knowledge of your own period. Surely the population problem was already phasing itself out at the time you went into hibernation."

"We considered it one of the most dangerous trends of our time."

"The existence of a trend doesn't mean it will continue, Jule. For instance, in the nineteenth century the horse population in the United States doubled, tripled, quadrupled at least every decade. But it slid to a halt shortly after the turn of the century, with the advent of the internal combustion engine. By the middle of the twentieth century, the horse was largely a rich man's hobby."

"That was horses. But in my day, human population was booming."

She shook her head. "It was already falling off in the most advanced countries. Japan and Holland were two of the first to achieve zero population growth, and West Germany, in 1972, was the first modern country to lose population: thirty-thousand to be exact. Even then the United States was pushing the zero population growth point. I'm no Marxist, but I go along with his materialist conception of history. Most of our institutions have economic backgrounds.''

''What in the devil has that got to do with the amount of population? By the way, how much larger is it now than it was in 1970?''

''I haven't seen recent statistics, but I assume it's smaller. There were too many people in the world for its resources.''

He just stared at her.

She explained impatiently, ''People of the past wanted large families to work on the farm, for child labor in factories, to help support the family. Especially in countries such as England; Marx's chapters on child labor in nineteenth century England are absolutely chilling. But by the twentieth century, what with developments in both industry and agriculture so that it was no longer practical to employ children—a child can't run a tractor, nor program a computer—families grew smaller. Particularly after women began to join the labor force. Women who worked were no longer in a position to raise children; well, not a whole brood of them, certainly. Houses and apartments were now rarely built with four or five bedrooms. And some landlords refused to take families with any children at all.

''Many women—as well as men—simply didn't want children. They would interfere with their lives, their jobs, their entertainment. Fun was no longer a matter of quilting parties, church socials, and candy pulls. Women wanted to be out and doing, as their husbands had been out and doing for a long time.''

"But it's an *instinct* to have children.''

"Yes, but not herds of them. In your day, a lot of people who had children didn't want them, couldn't afford them, couldn't support them. When the new, more efficient birth control devices came along about 1960, the growth rate slowed considerably. Today, you can have children or not, as you wish. We have perfect birth control methods for both men and women. One shot makes you sterile indefinitely. If you change your mind, another shot makes you fertile again within twenty-four hours. We also have very competent sexual instruction in our schools. In the mid-twentieth century literally millions of young people went into marriage each year without the vaguest idea of just what a sexual relationship consisted of, let alone how to avoid conception. Largely, of course, these were the uneducated, under-educated, and especially those of conservative religious backgrounds.''

Julian was on the defensive, though he wasn't sure why. He said, "Okay, that's the story in the advanced nations. What happened in India and China?''

"Roughly the same thing, but it came about a little later. In countries such as India, the original reason for an exploding population also ended. In the days of small farms, the parents wanted large families to help, and to take care of them when they grew too old to work. But the small farmer was getting squeezed out, and his children were going to the cities and the manufacturing centers. As a result, the children became a drain on their parents rather than a help. You conceived and raised a child until it was in its teens and then it disappeared. Obviously, it was less than profitable.

"China? They were in the forefront of limiting population. Their dictatorial bureaucracy soon realized that the nation could not allow a population boom. As far back as half a century ago, young people were not encouraged to marry until a minimum of twenty-five years of age. Birth control methods were made readily available and they were one of the first countries to institute free abortions for all."

They had finished their lunch and Edith put the dishes, utensils, napkins, etc. in the table center to sink away. When they went back into the living room, she sat down on the couch and Julian went over to the auto-bar. "Would you like a liqueur?" he asked.

"I'm not very keen on spirits, Jule."

"I can recommend Kahlua, if they have it in your liquor supplies. It's a Mexican drink based on coffee, and not too strong."

"They probably have it. I'll give it a try."

He ordered verbally into the screen and shortly two cordial glasses of the dark brown, thick drink arrived. He brought them over and sat near to her.

She sipped, and pronounced it delicious.

He said, "Our being on the subject of children and birth control and so forth brought back to me something that you said the other day. When I was—was proposing to you, after you said that you had gotten a teenage crush on me when you saw me in stasis in the hospital—under glass, so to speak . . ."

She smiled. "Yes?"

"You told me that you no longer had love. But that's ridiculous. The human race has always had love. Why, it's the finest of all emotions."

"You misunderstood. What I said was that we no longer had love as you used the word. The relationship between man and woman has evolved. Some of the older institutions, such as marriage, have all but disappeared; engagements, marriage, divorce have become antiquated. Primitive man didn't have marriage. It evolved when private ownership of property came along. A man wanted his property to descend to his own children, so he demanded that his wife be a virgin and, after marriage, sleep with no one but him. Strict laws were passed regulating marriage and the rights of men over women. But we have no private property now, beyond little personal things, so the need for either marriage or divorce has disappeared."

"But love. . . ?"

"Surprisingly enough, Jule, romantic love is a fairly recent development. The Crusaders, and especially the troubadours, brought it back with them to Europe from the Holy Land. If you remember your mythology, all that promiscuity and rape by the Greek gods and heroes could hardly be called love. It was simply lust or passion."

"But love . . ."

"Think about it, Julian, and you'll see how elastic a word it is. You love your mother, your father, your country, and possibly you love apple pie. Is that the same feeling you claim you have for me? Possibly you love a parade, too, but would you want to go to bed with one?''

''Well, you certainly haven't given up sex.''

''Of course not. It's one of the most important elements in life. We begin educating our children about sex as soon as they can comprehend it. I had my first sex tutor when I was fourteen.''

He looked at her with a complete lack of understanding. ''You had your first sex tutor at fourteen,'' he repeated uncomprehendingly.

''Yes, my first sex instructor.''

He imagined that he was still misunderstanding her. ''You mean actual instruction?''

''Yes. The age varies somewhat, since young people mature at different ages. I was fourteen when I applied for a sex tutor, after I had been medically checked out to see whether I was fully adult in my body's development; it's all done very carefully, since it's of so much importance. Then I had my hymen surgically removed and was given my birth control injection.''

''You had your hymen *removed*?''

''But certainly. Some girls have a great deal of difficulty the first time or two they have sexual intercourse if they have a strong hymen.''

He was staring outright at her. ''Just a minute, now. This sex tutor. Who assigns him to you?''

''Don't be ridiculous. I selected him myself from the volunteers available. Some sex instructors will have as many as four or five students.''

''All right. Then what happens?''

''Why, usually a girl goes out on a date with the

man she had decided to have as her tutor—or a boy with the woman he has selected—just to see if she really likes him and is attracted to him. If it turns out that she's made a suitable choice, the instruction begins."

"Where?"

"Why, at her home, or his, or at a hotel— wherever they choose."

"And what does he teach you?"

"Jule, I continually get the feeling that you aren't following me."

"And I continually get the feeling that every other sentence is being left out of this conversation."

She merely shrugged. "He teaches you sex. How to make love. How to have successful orgasms and multiple orgasms. How to have a successful sex life, in short."

"How long does this go on?" Julian managed to ask.

"As long as you still like him, or until you select a different tutor. Or until you've grown to the age when you want to make a more permanent arrangement with some man."

"And you had a sex tutor when you were only fourteen?"

"That's right. I had four altogether over several years. Then I met a boy I liked considerably and we moved in together. We were still students."

"And what happened to him?"

"He wanted to continue his studies in Guatemala and moved down there. I found another suitable fellow shortly afterwards. I think he was the best bed companion I've ever had."

"The same thing applies to boys as well?"

"Certainly."

"He picks a woman from among the volunteers and she teaches him how to——Listen, what kind of people would volunteer for that kind of work?".

"It's a great honor. Anyone who isn't so tied down to a permanent relationship, or whatever, and who likes sex especially well, will volunteer. They are usually at least twenty-five years of age and seldom over thirty-five. Everybody realizes how important sex education is, so the tutors are highly regarded. Some of them stay in the field for years but others drop out after a time. The Sexual Education Committee of a vicinity tries to select the most attractive-looking of the men and women who volunteer, so that the first sexual experiences of the young people will be as beautiful as possible."

He slumped back on the couch. "What a way to work out the problem." He looked at her again. "How many of these semi-permanent affairs have you had since you were fourteen?"

She shook her head as though surprised. "I don't know. I'm past twenty-five now. You don't remember how many women you've slept with, do you?"

"I suppose not. But in my day, we thought girls were different."

"Well, we're not."

Even as he stated it, the question sounded rather foolish, but out it came. "How do you strike up these semi-permanent affairs?"

She looked at him as though he wasn't being very bright. "Why, you meet somebody at a party, at a dance, possibly in a bar or some sports event, and if you're attracted to each other, you give it a try. If you like each other, you stay together as long as you wish.''

''But you don't get married?''

''A few do. Usually those who still have religious beliefs. But there is no civil connotation to the relationship. And no divorce is necessary. Either is free to walk out at will.''

''Suppose they have children?''

''Children are no longer dependent upon their parents. The children can go with one or the other, decide to spend six months with each, or go to a children's home and live there—whatever they wish.''

''You mean the poor kids are put in institutions?''

''Jule, Jule. . . . These institutions, as you call them, are all operated by people who love children the most and have been selected from the most suitable applicants——''

''By the computers, undoubtedly.'' He couldn't keep a sharp tone from his voice.

''Certainly. It's in their Aptitude Quotient. Some children prefer to apply for foster parents, and there are always more of those available than there are children to go around. People who love children but aren't capable of having them, for whatever reasons. Surely it was pretty much the same in your time.''

''We had orphans and people to adopt them,'' he said sourly. ''But some foster homes were in the racket for what they could get out of it. The State would put a kid in a foster home and pay the adults so much a month for their support.''

''That doesn't apply any longer, since the child in

this case has the same income as any adult."

Suddenly her eyes widened and she sat up straight. "Jule, you haven't had any sexual release since you've been revived, have you?"

He snorted. "Where in the hell would I get it?"

"Why, you poor man!" She leaned toward him and touched him in such a manner that he couldn't have been more surprised if she had suddenly sprouted a halo. "Why didn't you ask me?"

Then he had her in his arms. His mouth sought hers, and her lips were as soft as he had always known they would be.

He said, finally, "It never occurred to me. You said you'd had a teenage crush on me, but then when I told you I loved you, you said a permanent relationship between us was impractical."

"What has that got to do with enjoying ourselves in bed when we wish? You're very attractive to me, and you've already let me know you find me attractive—enough to have wanted to marry me. Now, come along. My bedroom is in here."

"At this time of day?" Though why he should protest he couldn't say.

She looked at him mockingly. "What's wrong with this time of day?"

Chapter Ten

The Year 1950

THEY MADE LOVE several times, and then, still nude, went into the kitchen and ate steaks washed down with dark, strong beer, which reminded him of the bock beers of Munich. Hand in hand, they returned to the bed, refreshed. The act of love was perfect with her. He had never bedded a more open woman. She was willing to try anything, and had quite a few tricks of her own that were new to him.

By the time they were completely satiated, it was dark, and she suggested that they spend the night and return to the university city in the morning.

"Don't you think you had better phone your people?"

"Sure, I'll do that right now."

By the time she returned to slip into bed next to him, he was dead asleep.

His dream about his first sexual experience was undoubtedly sparked by his lovemaking with Edith and by the discussion they'd had beforehand comparing the new sexual mores with the old.

Following a world cruise, which had turned out to be only a halfway-around-the-world cruise, after his revulsion to what he had seen in India, Julian had joined his uncle at his Catskill Mountains estate. For the first time in his life, he was enrolled at a public school: Kingston High School.

It was his own whim. His Uncle Albert had remonstrated mildly, pointing out that competent tutors were available at this stage of Julian's education if he wasn't interested in one of the better prep schools, but Julian had stuck to his guns. He was probably motivated by the desire to meet more people in his own age group, as there were few in his social class in the vicinity of Woodstock, the Catskill artist colony near which his uncle lived. So far as a prep school was concerned, he had been boarded out too many years of his life by his parents to desire that.

From the first, it was quite gratifying. He was a bit disconcerting for many of his teachers. He spoke better French than the French teacher, who had, admittedly never been to France, and German as well as the German instructor, which wasn't saying much. In geography, Julian had been to most of the countries studied, and in English literature the teacher was somewhat taken back to find that, among others, Julian knew Hemingway and Somerset Maugham quite well. In drama, he was well acquainted, personally, with Noel Coward, Orson Welles, John Gielgud, Lawrence Olivier, and a number of the more prominent cinema stars—all had often hosted, and been hosted by, the Wild Wests in their heyday.

But it was not his academic career that was his real forte so far as his contemporaries were concerned. He owned the largest Mercedes-Benz this side of Germany, and it was a sports model. It had formerly belonged to his father, who had raced it, and although it would be years before Julian came into his inheritance, his uncle had turned the vehicle over to him. In a school where those of his classmates who were fortunate enough to have a car at all drove jalopies, Julian was king.

Nor did his unlimited pocket money exactly turn him into a leper. Julian usually picked up the tab. Above that, his uncle's liquor cabinet was always available to him, and if his friends threw a party and wanted whiskey, gin, or whatever, Julian could always bring a couple of bottles.

Yes, Julian had become the rage of Kingston High School.

And particularly with the girls, who knew a good thing when they saw one. If there was a single girl in the school who would not have given her all to make Julian West her steady, she wasn't evident.

Of these, Peggy Ten Eyck, daughter of a Kingston small shop proprietor, was among the most lush. Blonde and blue-eyed in the Dutch tradition, mature figure, beautiful legs, an instinctively good dresser, Peggy had cut her own swath through the male students before Julian's arrival. But one look at that Mercedes-Benz and all the other boys were left in the dust.

His dream began with his picking her up at dusk at the drugstore, which was the school hangout, and speeding out of town with the top down, the wind streaming her hair out behind her. As soon as they crossed the bridge and were on the road to West Hurley and Woodstock beyond, Julian released the horses. Though he had learned to drive years before, sitting on his father's lap, it had only been a year that he had been able to do as much of it as he liked.

The car sprang forward and Peggy Ten Eyck gasped.

She said, "Golly, Jule, aren't you afraid some motorcycle cop might come along?"

He laughed exuberantly at the speed. It was a beautiful June evening, as only the Catskills can provide. The sun had just set behind Overlook Mountain, and the coloring of the sky blended with the new dark green of the hills.

"My uncle's in good with the county commissioner," he told her. "They know better than to bother me. A couple of times they've tried. I just turn the ticket over to Uncle Albert."

"Wow," she said, impressed. She put one hand to her hair, an attempt to keep it in some semblance of order, and looked at him out the side of her eyes.

His sport jacket had been tailored of Donegal tweed, in Ireland; his shirt of Egyptian cotton had come from Paris; his cravat, tailored slacks and his shoes were bought in London. He wasn't particularly aware of these facts. He had always been outfitted in the same shops as his father, and had accepted without much thought the reality of owning nothing but the best in haberdashery, suits and sport clothing.

To small-town Peggy Ten Eyck, he cut a breathtaking figure.

His face and body, in its new manhood, did not detract from the picture. He had reached his full height, just short of six feet, and weighed approximately one-hundred sixty-five pounds. He had the good carriage of one who has been well trained to horses at an early age. His hair was dark and slightly curly, and his face aristocratically handsome.

To Peggy Ten Eyck he was everything Hollywood had ever promised.

They sped up the highway, which was largely deserted at this time of day, reached West Hurley and cut off on the narrower road toward Woodstock.

"Where are we going, Jule?" Peggy gasped into the wind.

"I'll never tell."

She giggled.

They slowed as they passed the Woodstock summer theatre and the Big Deep swimming hole on the edge of town. Julian eased up still more as they passed Deanie's restaurant and the town square. He was a fast driver, given the proper conditions, but his father had also schooled him well in safety in motoring.

"We can come back later for a bite at Deanie Elwyn's," Julian told her.

"Wonderful," Peggy said. "I just love his hamburgers."

Julian snorted. "He has better food than that," he told her. They had reached the edge of the art colony and he sped up again on the way to Lake Hill.

Just short of the town, Julian said, "Ah, here we are," and came nearly to a halt, then turned off on a dirt road, which led steeply upward.

"Where in the world are we going?" she asked, no apprehension whatsoever in her voice.

"To the prettiest maple grove I've ever run into," he told her. "I found it by accident, just driving around on the back roads, kind of exploring. Some day we'll have to get the gang together and have a picnic. Possibly in the fall, when the leaves begin to turn."

"Sounds awfully romantic," Peggy said, looking at him again from the side of her eyes.

He pulled the car off to the side, into a mountain glen which was everything he had described. There was even a small stream at the far side, running clear with mountain water.

He stopped the car and turned off the engine.

"Isn't this something?"

Peggy turned to him. At the age of fourteen and a half, Peggy Ten Eyck had never been out with a boy who hadn't attempted to kiss her as soon as he was able to get her alone. She had no doubt in the world that it had been Julian's intent in bringing her here.

As a matter of fact, though, it hadn't. He had brought her for the reason he had said: to show her the maple grove as a site for a future picnic. Julian was not unkissed, but he had never felt he had to prove his developing manhood by kissing every girl at every opportunity that presented itself. In the atmosphere he had been raised in, sex was not a desperate thing—there was too much of it around.

She tipped her head.

Julian was a gentleman born and raised. He couldn't disappoint a lady. Besides, he considered her the prettiest girl in Kingston High School, which boasted some two thousand students.

So he kissed her. Perhaps it was the balmy beauty of the evening, perhaps it was the romantic setting. Perhaps it was two teenagers only recently having become aware of the sexual urge. But he had never been so stirred by a kiss. Her mouth was soft; her mouth was willing; her mouth was hot. Her mouth demanded more, and he gave it to her.

She moved against him, and he could feel her breasts. They were surprisingly mature breasts, considering her age. Something he had once heard his father say came back to him. *They're big enough when they're old enough and they're old enough when they're big enough.* At the time the meaning had eluded him, but he understood now.

Young people can spend hours kissing, but on this occasion passion was mounting rapidly to higher levels. Julian tentatively cupped one of the ample breasts with his left hand.

Her mouth still glued to his, she squirmed and murmured, "You mustn't do that."

Julian responded to the protest by ignoring it.

They continued to kiss. Through her blouse and brassiere he could feel her nipple stiffening and it excited him—to the point where he could feel himself rapidly acquiring an erection. It had happened to him on necking binges before, so he wasn't surprised.

He took his hand and slipped it into the neck of her blouse.

"Oh, no," she murmured, her voice low and sexy-tinged.

He obeyed her no more than he had before. He

fondled her breast for a moment over the brassiere, and then slipped his hand inside. He was enjoying himself immensely.

Her breath was coming deeper.

He whispered, "Let me kiss you there."

"Oh, no!"

"Just once. You're so beautiful."

"Oh, I couldn't."

"Please."

Peggy had had her breasts kissed before by boys not even near Julian's class. She said demurely, "Just a minute."

She unbuttoned her blouse and wriggled her hand up her back to unsnap her brassiere. This was going as well as her fondest hope. She had long schemed to get Julian alone somewhere—anywhere—so she could prove to him that she was worthy to be his steady.

The brassiere fell away and Julian was confronted with the most beautiful sight he had ever seen. He bent his lips worshipfully, and feasted on the pinkness of the cherrystone nipple.

"Oh," she moaned.

Julian had gone beyond the point of no return. Surreptitiously, he unzipped his pants. The night, now, was quite dark. He reached out and took her hand and put it on his penis, continuing to kiss her nipple.

At first she obviously didn't know what it was she was holding, but then suddenly she stiffened. Her grasp too stiffened, so that she held it tightly. She let go in quick alarm and tried to sit up and away from him.

"What's the matter?" he asked, his voice husky.

"I . . . I think we better go now."

"Why?"

"Well . . . I . . . I've never done this before."

"Oh, come on now."

"Well, I haven't."

"Are you chicken?"

She said, only half angrily, "No, I'm not. But I promised my mother I'd never do it until I got married."

"Oh, great," he said, the terms of seduction coming to him instinctively. "I'm not even in college yet, and you want to be married."

There was a long moment of silence. This was the most handsome boy she had ever met in her life, and the most gentlemanly; he even talked like he was an Englishman or something. He never swore; he was never gauche (the word wasn't part of her vocabulary, of course). Above all, she knew that he was going to inherit one of the largest fortunes in the United States. What it boiled down to was, *he's the richest guy I'm ever going to meet.*

She said cautiously, "Well, I know we can't be married now. But if you really love me, we could be kind of engaged, go steady and all."

"Of course," he said, reaching for her breasts again. It was not part of his real nature to lie, but . . .

She said worriedly, "I . . . I don't know much about it. I've never done it."

Inwardly, he doubted it, in spite of her age. He himself was a virgin but, somehow or other, he believed that Peggy couldn't be. If she were a virgin, a "good girl," why had she let him go this far?

The seat of the Mercedes-Benz was ample but it would have taken a more experienced seducer than the young Julian to have figured out the mechanics of what he was attempting.

He had his left hand up her skirt now, fumbling at the hem of her briefs. He had never gone any further than this with a girl but he knew that tonight he was going to. He hesitantly ran his hand over her, and clumsily tried to insert his finger.

"Oh, no," she said. "I . . . I've changed my mind. I guess I'd better go home. I've never done it. I . . ."

He ignored her.

After a few more moments of being mauled, she said, "Let me take my panties off."

He acceded to that and drew away long enough for her to arch her hips and pull down her nylon briefs. His mouth was dry and his breath was coming in pants.

She left her skirt halfway up to her hips. "Do you love me, Jule?"

"Of course," he told her, trying to get her arranged with her back between the seat and the door so that he could mount her. He pressed against her, seeking entrance.

She gasped, "How much do you love me?"

There was no answer.

She said, "Oh, be careful, that hurts."

"Only for a minute," he said. "It hurts only for a minute." He knew now that she hadn't been lying. She, too, was a virgin.

"Oh," she said, "be careful. That hurts bad. I . . . I've never done it before."

He was in a rage of passion now, though trying to listen to her and be careful. He jabbed, jabbed again.

"Oh, Jule, that's not the place. I don't think that's the place. Oh, that hurts."

He rubbed against her frantically. He simply *had* to get inside her. He poked and pushed.

"Oh, no," she gasped. "That hurts awful. Don't do that."

"I have to," he groaned, straining against her.

"Something's wrong," she said. "You're not doing it right. Haven't you ever done it before?"

"No," he muttered, straining still.

"I . . . I think we better stop. What you're doing hurts awful."

"No!"

And then he came, all over her. He gasped, then moaned.

She said, "What . . . what happened?"

Julian was definitely embarrassed. "I . . . I just, uh, they call it *came*."

"Oh," Peggy said. She knew what the word meant. "You mean you're all through?" There was relief in her voice.

"I . . . I guess so. I'm sorry. Did I hurt you?"

"Not very much. I, well, I don't think you were doing it right. I don't think you really . . . did me. Not completely."

"I don't think so either," he said, a feeling of inadequacy coming over him.

She asked, "Do you have a handkerchief?"

He fished out his white linen handkerchief and handed it over.

"I'm sorry," he said again. He rezipped his pants, averting his eyes from her attempt to clean herself up.

She slipped back into her briefs. With as much

embarrassment as he himself was feeling, she said, "That didn't work very well, did it? Maybe next time we can be in a bed or something. And . . . well, shouldn't you have one of those rubber things or something?"

"Yeah," he said, disgusted with the whole thing.

Suddenly the beam of a flashlight was on them and a gruff voice said, "Okay, you two, what goes on?"

The newcomer was in uniform.

Julian said, "We were just parked here enjoying the evening, Officer."

"Oh, yeah? Then how come her skirt is halfway up to her belly button?"

Julian sighed and lifted out his wallet. He selected a twenty-dollar bill, and proffered it, saying, "I'm Julian West, Officer. It is a pleasure to meet you. The young lady and I were doing a bit of . . . necking. I'm sure you understand. Please have a beer on me at your favorite tavern."

"Oh," the other said. "You're Mr. West's nephew?"

"That is correct, Officer."

The man, who had already taken the bill, tipped a finger to his cap. "Sorry to have bothered you. Have a good time, sir."

"Golly," Peggy said when he was gone. "I was afraid he'd run us in. It's lucky he didn't come up five minutes ago."

"It wouldn't have made any difference," Julian said wearily, reaching for the car key.

The dream ended at that point, and Julian came awake to find Edith sleeping beside him, a deep gentle sleep of complete relaxation and health.

As he lay there, the rest of the sordid experience come back to him. He had never gone out with Peggy again. Somehow or other, he couldn't bring himself to face her. Besides, shortly afterward he had met an older and considerably more experienced woman who had efficiently introduced him to the pleasures to be found in bed.

It was approximately seven months later that his uncle, a glint of amusement in his eye, said, "Did you know that you were about to become a father?"

Julian froze.

Albert West laughed. He went over to the sideboard and took up a bottle of the Scotch he had specially imported from Glenlivet, and splashed two generous portions into tall highball glasses. He returned to where his nephew sat and handed him a drink.

He said, "Mr. Ten Eyck was over this morning. He wants you to marry the girl—for which I don't blame him, considering your financial position. Is the child yours?"

Julian knocked back some of the liquor. "No!" he said.

"You're sure?"

"Yes."

"She says it is."

Julian shook his head emphatically. "No. I was necking with her and tried to, but it didn't work. I never went out with her again."

"According to her doctor, the child was conceived in August."

"The only time I ever went out with her was in

June, last June. What can we do? I mean . . . what can I do?''

His uncle laughed and winked at him. ''It's already been done, Jule.''

''What do you mean?''

''I pointed out to Mr. Ten Eyck that you were in London in August. All of August.''

''But I wasn't, Uncle Albert. I was right here in Woodstock.''

''Yes, but can they prove it?''

''There must be people who could testify that I was here.''

The older man took a pull at his whiskey. ''And I can get letters from London testifying that you were there. For instance, I could get a statement from the Duke and Duchess that you were a house guest of theirs. Whose testimony, here in Ulster County, would stand up to that? If necessary, I know a chief steward on the French Line who would gladly do me the favor of testifying that you were a passenger on his ship, both going and returning, during the period involved.''

Julian stared at him.

His uncle laughed again. ''I gave Ten Eyck a check and told him to send the girl away for a few months. If they had come to me sooner, she could have had an abortion, but it's too late for that now. See here, my boy, you're getting to the age where you're going to have to watch out for these things. Every woman you run into is going to have her eye on the West fortune. To be safe, why don't you let me set up a little flat or house in Kingston for you? I'll check with Polly Adler down in the city and we'll arrange for a nice experienced girl to take it over. You can visit her when you, ah, have the urge.''

Julian experienced a great inner relief, but he said, ''No thanks, Uncle Albert.''

''Suit yourself, but don't worry about Ten Eyck. I warned him that if he took this to court, I'd hire the best lawyers in the state to defend you. And that when the case fell through, I'd prosecute both him and his daughter.''

It was the first time his family's money had been ruthlessly utilized to protect him from his actions.

Chapter Eleven

The Year 2, New Calendar

In the three short decades between now and the twenty-first century, millions of ordinary, psychologically normal people will face an abrupt collision with the future. Citizens of the world's richest and most technologically advanced nations, many of them, will find it increasingly painful to keep up with the incessant demand for change that characterizes our time. For them, the future will have arrived too soon.
— Alvin Toffler, *Future Shock*

HE REALIZED THAT Edith had opened her eyes and was watching him with an expression compounded of sleepiness, warmth, satisfaction, affection . . . and possibly a bit of humor.

He said, wiping his dream thoughts of Peggy Ten Eyck from his mind, "Good morning, Edie."

"Good morning, darling. Did I make you happy?"

He took in her beauty. During past sexual experiences he had most often dreaded seeing his bed companion in the harshness of morning light; makeup smeared, hair a mop, breath heavy with the tobacco and alcohol of the night before, the animal smell of used sex and dried sweat. It didn't apply to Edith Leete. She had never worn cosmestics in her life, her hair was short cut, she neither smoked nor drank beyond a bit of wine or beer with meals. And now that he thought about it, after their last bout with Eros, she had gone into the bath and showered. He was disgusted with himself for not having done the same.

Now she was fresh and beautiful.

He nodded and said, "Yes. Yes, Edie."

"All right, then. Breakfast. Last one up is a rotten egg!" She threw back the single sheet that covered them and began to swing her excellent legs over the side of the bed.

He said, "Wait just a minute."

She looked at him and raised her eyebrows mockingly. "What? After all that? Are you a satyr?"

He shook his head this time. "No. It's not that. I just wanted to look at you, and perhaps ... tell you I love you."

Her eyes had narrowed very slightly and there was something possibly sad behind them. But her words came out in a laugh. "You are—what was your old term?—*corny*," she told him.

He protested, "I'm not that old. Between that word and the time I went into hibernation there was 'square,' 'not with it,' 'not hep,' and various others I can't think of right now. But, okay, breakfast it is."

They took turns in the bath and when he returned to the bedroom she had already garbed herself in the dungarees she almost always affected, and had dialed a complete new outfit for him except for shoes. He found it difficult to get used to the modern custom of wearing clothes a single time and then disposing of them to be recycled. He had been told that less labor was involved in such a system than washing, drying, ironing, replacing buttons, mending tears and holes. The textile industry was one of the most highly automated in the nation.

They headed for the kitchen. On the way, Edith said, "Jule, tell me about prostitutes."

"What?"

"About prostitutes. Whores."

As they sat down at the kitchenette table, he asked, "What's this fascination you women have with the subject? Your mother asked me about it just the other day."

"A double order of ham and eggs, lots of toast, butter, marmalade? A liter of coffee?"

"I could use it," he agreed emphatically.

After she dialed, she said, "From this perspective in time, it's almost impossible to understand it, though, of course, as a student of anthropology I realize that since history began, prostitution existed in most parts of the world. But why did they do it?"

"For money," he said, his voice laconical.

"How much money did they get?"

He rubbed his forehead thoughtfully. "I suppose it depended on the country, how attractive they were, how young. I've heard of prices ranging from twenty-five cents to five hundred dollars."

"Twenty-five cents!"

"Women in India, aged, half-starved, undoubtedly diseased."

"And five hundred dollars?"

The food had arrived. After she served it, he said, "In places such as New York, Hollywood, Paris, and London, they had ultra-swank call girls. Very high-class office, usually under the guise of a model agency or some such. You had to be properly introduced, properly identified, and all the rest of it. For anywhere from two hundred dollars up you could have a girl for the evening who was very presentable, well educated, a good conversationalist, and supremely attractive. The five-hundred-dollar ones were usually recognizable TV or movie starlets, who even gave you a bit of prestige when seen with them in the top nightspots or restaurants. Few people knew, of course, that they augmented their incomes by putting out for their arranged dates at an agreed-upon price."

"They must have hated it."

"To the contrary, some of them loved it. I recall once being invited on a yachting cruise with five other upper-class chaps in roughly my own age group. There were eight girls aboard, all of them available at any time. The party lasted a week. The best of food, the best of booze, and, frankly, the best of girls. They were all college students, by the way, making a bit of extra cash during the summer. Believe me, if there were any of them that didn't love the job, they didn't show it. As I recall, the yacht owner gave them a thousand dollars apiece at the end of the cruise. On top of that, some of the rest of us tipped their favorites."

She shook her head in disbelief, even as she ate.

"But basically, how degrading."

He shrugged. "There were male prostitutes too. Handsome young physical specimens whom older women, usually, would go for—either for one-night stands, indefinite arrangements, or sometimes marriage."

She shook her head again. "I can't imagine such a code of sexual morality."

He had to laugh at that. "Well, it's a little difficult for me to comprehend some aspects of yours."

"I read that a good many of these women were lesbians; that they came to hate men so much that they turned to women for their real sexual release."

"Evidently some were. I think more were bisexual. There was quite a book on it just before I went under. *The Happy Hooker*. The author was a top-paid prostitute and madam who liked both men and women. Are there more lesbians now, since you've let down the legal barriers against homosexuals so far as consenting adults are concerned?"

"Oh, no. I would think considerably less. It turned out that in many cases it was largely psychological—not completely, of course—and most of it disappeared among both men and women when legal restraints were removed and sex education improved. I tried it once."

He eyed her in surprise. "You did?"

"Uh huh," she said around a mouthful of ham. "Just to see what it was like. With a girl friend at school. I didn't like it, though. I like men."

"So I noticed," he said.

"What was swinging all about?" she asked.

"Swingers? Oh, well, toward the end of the sixties or so, a lot of sexual restraints were lifting. Quite a few people, especially the younger ones, were experimenting. Sometimes whole groups would get together and with complete abandon have any type of sex they could think of."

"Single people or married couples?"

"Both. Sometimes they'd have little clubs, sort of, that would consist of two, three or four, or even more married couples who would meet weekly and have a sexual binge. Everyone who participated was expected to, uh, put out for anyone who wanted him or her. The others could stand around and watch or, if aroused, join in."

"Were you ever at one of these parties?"

"To tell the truth, no. It never appealed to me."

"It doesn't appeal to me, either. I think sex is a very personal thing between two people. Speaking as an anthropologist, offhand I can't think of any society where group sex seemed to develop." She considered it for a moment, before adding, "Unless you count some of the orgiastic religious mysteries of, say, the early Greeks. And they were invariably performed while under some hallucinogen such as the *amanita muscaria* sacred mushrooms. How do you account for it in your time?"

He cocked his head slightly. "I suppose it was just one more aspect of the revolt that was going on, especially among the young. One group or another was protesting just about every aspect of our society. I suppose the swingers were protesting the restraints that had been put on sex for so long. Then, of course, there was wife-swapping."

She looked at him.

He cleared his throat. "Two or more couples

would get together periodically and exchange wives for the night, or for a weekend, or whatever."

"Then why bother to get married at all?"

"Darned if I know. There were a lot of books and magazine articles by sociologists and others digging into the phenomenon. Some were pro and some were con. But I didn't read anything that made sense to me particularly. At the time, as you know, I was preparing to be married myself, and would have been horrified by the idea of swapping my wife with someone else." He grinned ruefully. "However, you know, in spite of the fact that I was the son of the Wild Wests—or possibly *because* of it—I was slightly on the prudish side when it came to such things."

They had finished their breakfast.

She asked nonchalantly, "Would you like to go back to bed for just a little, before we return to the university?"

They didn't get back to the Julian West University City until past lunch. They had stopped on the way at a motel which boasted an automated restaurant. Julian hadn't noted any lessening in the food quality, which is something he could hardly have said about the food in roadside restaurants of his own era.

He kept thinking of these days as other than his own time, which, in a way, was ridiculous. But a third of a century had passed, of which he had no memories whatsoever.

As they rode up in the elevator Edith murmured, "Father will be furious with me."

Then it hit him. A guest of the Leetes, so greatly in the debt of the doctor and his wife, he had taken the first opportunity to bed their daughter. He closed his eyes in pain. What kind of a bastard was he?

"I . . . I suppose there's no excuse," he said. "I hate to deliberately lie to the Academician and your mother. After all, we were gone all night, and they aren't stupid."

She frowned at him. "What is there to lie about?"

He stared back at her. "You said he would be furious at our sleeping together."

"That's not what I said at all. I said he would be furious."

He was even more confused. "What will he be furious about?"

"That I took so long to see that you——"

"You mean your parents won't *care*?"

"Why in the world should they? You're in your mid-thirties, I'm in my mid-twenties, and we like each other. Isn't it expected that we have sexual appetites? At present, I have no man I've been seeing regularly—or irregularly, for that matter. And, of course, you have met so few outside our family that you haven't had much opportunity. In fact, have you met any young women at all?"

"One or two, on my way in or out of the building."

"Well, were any of them attractive?"

He thought about the girl of whom he had asked directions to the Cub Bar. "I suppose so."

"You could have asked one of them," she said. "They would have undoubtedly been fascinated to sleep with Julian West. Why didn't you?"

He said sourly, "Because I didn't want a bust on the nose."

"Why in the world would she want to put her breasts on your nose?"

"Never mind," he told her. "You're not completely up on the idiom of my day."

They had reached their floor. Julian left Edith at the door to the Leete apartment.

He said, "I think I'll go on back to my own place and pick up a few notes I made before you told me about using the data banks. Unless you have something on, I'll be over shortly."

"Fine, darling." She offered her lips for a quick kiss, and he took immediate advantage of the opportunity before taking off.

He hadn't the vaguest idea of where he stood with her. Had they just had a one-night stand, or was she willing to go into what she called a semi-permanent relationship? He hoped it was the latter. She had mentioned that at present she had no young man. Her parting kiss and the casual endearment might be a good sign.

He entered and headed directly to his study. At the threshold, he stopped dead. Even at a distance, it was obvious to him that the room had been searched. He was immaculate so far as keeping his things in order. Even before he crossed to the desk, he knew very well that his notes had been gone through; they simply were not in the order in which he had left them.

He stared down at the desk for long moments.

Possibly the doctor, or even his wife, had found some reason to come over and, in curiosity, had looked through the notes he had made while studying. It didn't seem very likely but, on the other hand, he knew practically no one else. In the past month, the doctor had introduced him to a few cut-and-dried types connected with the "Julian West Project," other doctors or academicians of one sort or another, but he could not imagine that any one of them would have entered his apartment and gone through his things.

He went into the other rooms. Nothing seemed to have been disturbed. For that matter, the few things he had brought with him from the past were those that he carried in his pockets. He hadn't even gotten around, as yet, to securing a few items in the way of art objects and handicrafts to personalize his quarters, although both Edith and Martha had promised to help him to that end.

It was simply a mystery.

He shrugged it off, found the notes he had wanted to ask the Leetes about, and left for their apartment.

In spite of the fact Edie had assured him that the doctor would in no way object to Julian sleeping with his daughter, he was still embarrassed about facing him. He knew he was probably being foolish. If the girl had received instruction from a sex tutor at the age of fourteen and on, and had had a whole series of affairs since then. . . . But still . . .

He stood before the identity screen of the Leete apartment and the door swung open. He entered the living room, stepping into what seemed an intense conversation between the academician and his daughter.

They looked up at his approach.

"I'm not intruding, am I?" he said hurriedly, already turning to leave.

"No, no, of course not," Leete told him. "It's just that I had another strange experience this morning."

Julian stopped in his tracks.

The doctor said slowly, "I went out for a drive through the countryside, just to gather my thoughts about a project I've been involved in for some time. I was on manual control, of course, most of the surface roads not being automated as yet. When a car pulled up behind me, I edged over to the side of the road to let it pass. However, it didn't pass. I slowed. It slowed. There were four men in it. I couldn't make them out very well, but they all seemed to be somewhat young. Still not thinking it overly strange, I sped up. They sped up and deliberately hit my rear bumper, an action that wasn't particularly safe at that speed."

"Jesus Christ!" said Julian.

The other went on, "Somewhat shocked now, I sped up still more, and they continued to pursue. In my rear view mirror I could see that the two in the front seat were laughing. I tried everything I could think of; I turned down smaller side roads, thinking that they would continue on the highway, but they didn't. They kept following, bumping my rear bumper at every opportunity. I was terrified that I might turn over. My car was an open one; theirs wasn't."

"Good heavens, Father," Edith exclaimed. "Why didn't you summon Highway Security?"

He looked at her strangely. "I couldn't. My car phone wouldn't work. They pursued me a good many kilometers before finally dropping away and abandoning the chase. I returned immediately and confronted one of the mechanics at the car pool. He examined the vehicle that I had taken over and, his face set in amazement, said that the car phone had been tampered with. I simply can't understand it. And one other thing that would seem impossible . . .''

He reached into a side pocket and brought forth a piece of paper, handing it first to Julian. ''I found this in my pocket, after I got back here to the apartment.''

Julian scowled down at it. ''. . . one must either anticipate change or be its victim. —John K. Galbraith.''

Julian handed the paper to Edith. As she read it, he asked, ''Could someone have slipped it into your pocket down in the lobby, or coming up in the elevator?''

''Why . . . I suppose so,'' the older man said, scowling. ''I probably nudged against people all the way up from the car pool.''

Julian slumped into a chair. He suspected that he was more at home in this atmosphere than were these other two, who had lived in a sheltered society for the past thirty years.

He took a deep breath and said, ''Look, in this Republic of the Golden Rule society of yours, are there many malcontents?''

They didn't quite understand him at first.

He said impatiently, ''I know this is Utopia, but there must be some who are dragging their heels. Even in Heaven there was a revolt of the angels and they had to kick Lucifer and some of the boys out.''

Leete scowled. ''We keep telling you, Julian: this is not Utopia. There is no such thing as Utopia. Society is in a continual condition of flux. Of course there are malcontents in United America today.''

''Who are they?''

152

He thought about that. "There are various individuals and groups. For instance, some of those who were at the very top under the former socioeconomic system; some of the ultra-wealthy; some of the former politicians who wielded great power and loved it."

Edith said, "Some of the military, especially the top brass. But also lower echelons of the military who liked it for its own sake—its discipline, its traditions of glory."

"I see what you mean," Julian muttered. "If George Armstrong Custer or old Blood-and-Guts George Patton were alive today, they'd hate a world in which there was no longer the need for war."

Leete added, "Quite a few of the religious, too. They rebel against the fact that religion is so rapidly disappearing under this socioeconomic system."

That surprised Julian. "You mean that you can't study religion any more?"

"No, no. I don't mean that at all. A student can study religion, any religion. But we no longer teach religion as though it were true. If you decide that anything from the Amish to Zoroastrianism is the true faith, then you're certainly free to embrace its teachings. But we don't teach religion as *religion*. As the old expression goes, we let everyone go to hell in his own way. Some of the more orthodox—the Fundamentalists, the Roman Catholics, the Orthodox Jews—object. Younger people in our society don't pay much attention to religion, which infuriates the generations which were raised in it."

"Who else?" Julian asked grimly.

Both Edith and the doctor thought for awhile.

Edith said, "There are some who strongly object to the fact that two percent of the population is all that is needed to produce what we need. Many of these, too, are members of the old religions, such as the Seventh Day Adventists. The Bible says that man was meant to earn his bread by the sweat of his brow; today, nobody need sweat any more. Surprisingly enough, a good many of these objectors are among the ninety-eight percent who don't work and subsist on their Guaranteed Annual Income. I suppose they are the ones who can find no manner in which to fill their leisure time profitably."

Julian grunted.

Leete said slowly, "In actuality, there are quite a few of the older people, those in their sixties and beyond, who are taken aback by the many changes and long for the old ways. They haven't kept up with the changes, and the so-called generation gap hits them the hardest. They rebel against everything from the new way of schooling to the new sexual permissiveness. They object to the fact that drugs are no longer controlled, or to pornography being freely available to anyone silly enough to want to read it. Some even protest that there is no longer news censorship on any level."

"All right," Julian said. "Most of those you've mentioned belong to the older generations. Time has passed them by and they're uncomfortable. How about dissident groups among the younger people?"

Edith was obviously the one to answer that. She said, her voice unhappy, "Some of our youth, usually those of too low an Aptitude Quotient to be selected by the computers for a job on Muster Day, read the old stories and look at the old movies and TV shows in the International Data Banks and become enamored of the past. They seem to think present-day life is static and unadventurous."

Her father said sourly, "When I was a youngster, I used to dream of the days when knights were bold and damsels swooned. It never occurred to me that during the Dark Ages not one person out of a hundred was a knight or a damsel. Ninety-nine percent of the population were out in the fields, serfs grubbing away at the soil with primitive tools."

"Who else?" Julian demanded. "Who else in this Utopia of yours wants change?"

Both of them thought for long moments, and finally both shook their heads.

Julian said, "In my day, and before it, there were people, most of whom were probably very idealistic, who were nevertheless rebels. They existed in just about every country, and in every socioeconomic system. I guess you could say they were *re-volutionists*. People in my position were inclined to believe these types to be crackpots, or opportunists. But most of them were not. Tom Paine, for instance, who probably more than any other single person put over the American Revolution of 1776, was neither a crackpot nor personally ambitious. Neither was Lenin or Trotsky. Neither was Mao or Che Guevara. Who else can I think of who wasn't grinding his own ax? Let's say Jean-Paul Marat, of the French Revolution; Rosa Luxemberg, the German radical following the First World War; the anarchist, Kropotkin. Let's say Wendell Phillips, the American abolitionist."

Both Leete and Edith were frowning at him.

"I fail to see your point," the academician said.

Julian took a breath. "It would seem that in any socioeconomic system there are what can only be described as instinctive revolutionists. I'm not talking about the Hitlers, the Mussolinis, the Francos, I mean the idealistically motivated—whether they are right or wrong in their beliefs. Karl Marx was neither a villain nor a fool, but he was a lifelong revolutionist. Do you have any equivalent today?"

Leete slumped back in his chair. "Why . . . why, I don't know. I suppose that possibly we have. I wouldn't agree with them, but that doesn't mean that I don't admit their right to disagree with our present social system."

Julian wryly misquoted, "I thoroughly disagree with what you have to say, and would defend with my life your right to say it."

Edith asked, "What are you leading up to, Jule?"

He shook his head, then motioned to the doctor to follow him.

Leete, mystified, let his guest lead him to the bathroom. There, Julian turned on both the shower and the faucet in the lavatory.

He whispered, "Keep your voice low."

The doctor stared at him, but nodded.

Julian whispered, "Do you know what a bug is?"

"A bug?"

"A device that can be put into your home, or in your phone screen, to listen in on everything you say."

Leete was still gawking at him. "You mean like in that Watergate scandal way back?" he whispered.

"Never heard of it," Julian whispered. "Must

have happened after I went into stasis."

"Why, yes, but we haven't had anything like that for——"

"As you say, but could some of them be left over, here or there, or would there be plans on how to make them in the International Data Banks?"

Leete nodded dumbly. "Everything is in the data banks."

"Okay. Are there plans there to make a mop?"

"What's a mop?"

"An electronic device utilized to detect bugs."

They were both still whispering over the sound of the rushing water. "Why, I suppose so."

Next, Julian asked, "Do you have a friend who could get the plans out of the data banks and have a mop made secretly?"

"I suppose any of my friends who have hobby electronic shops in their basements or wherever could do it, particularly if the things go back over thirty years. It should be child's play for a modern electronic tinkerer."

"Somebody you could absolutely trust to secrecy?"

Leete thought, then nodded.

"All right. Get at it immediately," Julian snapped. "Now, one other thing. Are you connected with the government in any way?"

"How did you know? I am associated with a committee which is working upon suggestions for reforming our present civil branch of the government. As you know, our present system is dual, one pertaining to economic matters, production and distribution, and the other to civic matters, the equivalent of what the government was in the old days. Under the revised constitution——"

"Okay, okay," Julian interrupted. "Let's go back to the living room. Don't say anything, anything at all about this to anyone. Not even Martha or Edith."

The doctor gaped at him all over again, but nodded agreement.

Chapter Twelve

The Year 2, New Calendar

The Law, in its majestic equality, forbids the rich as well as the poor to sleep under bridges, to beg in the streets, and to steal bread.
—Anatole France

I'm anti-communists! What more do they want of me?
—Anthony Anastasia, Mafia Godfather

America is beginning to accept a new code of ethics that allows for chiseling and lying.
—Walter Lippmann

WHEN THE TWO MEN reentered the room Edith looked at them questioningly. "What have you two been up to?"

"I'll never tell," Julian said, doing his best to leer.

The doctor went over to the phone screen.

Julian said hurriedly, "Who are you going to call?"

"Why, that friend I just told you about."

Julian shook his head. "Go and see him."

Leete looked mildly surprised, but then nodded. "I see," he said.

"Yes. And keep obviously what is in mind, in mind," Julian insisted, and then added somewhat wearily, "I am from an age when we were conscious of these things."

"What in heaven are you two talking about?" Edith demanded.

"A dirty joke," Julian said.

"What is a dirty joke?"

He looked at her in exasperation. "See here," he said. "Ever since I came out of stasis, you've been telling me we don't have this any more, you don't have banks, you don't have cities in the sense we had them a third of a century ago. You don't have wars, and you don't have jails. You don't have newspapers and you don't have schools in the sense that we did. You don't even have stores. But now I am calling a halt. Don't tell me you don't tell dirty stories any more!"

Doctor Leete was chuckling. He said, "You know, it's been so long that I'd just about forgotten. Dirty stories were simply stories usually based on taboos such as sex, or excretion, and usually involving taboo words. Do away with the taboos and the institution disappears."

Edith was mystified. "What's a taboo word?"

Julian was looking from one to the other. He had been in stasis for something like ten years before Edith had even been born.

The academician laughed again. "I doubt if any

explanation would make sense to you. When I was a lad, I could say 'pee', if I meant urinate, but if I said 'piss,' I was spanked.''

Julian chimed in, ''I was allowed to say 'heck,' but if I said 'hell,' I was punished, although the word was used in the same way. Some parents were even more strict. Their children could say 'Gad,' but not 'God.' 'Goddamnit' came out 'gaddarnit.'''

''What has all this got to do with dirty jokes, whatever they are?''

Julian sighed. ''Let me think of an example. Okay. An American was telling an Englishman a poem:

Mary had a little skirt
　Slit right up the side
And every time she took a step
　It showed her little thigh.

''The Englishman returned to London and told it to a friend:

Mary had a little skirt
　Split right up the front
And every time she took a step
　It showed her little . . . no, that can't be right.''

The doctor laughed mildly but Edith merely looked at Julian and said, ''That's a dirty story?''

''Well, yes.''

''A joke?''

''Yes.''

''What's funny about it?''

Julian closed his eyes in pain. ''It's like your father

was telling you: it's based on a taboo word. So the Englishman by suggesting it, though not actually saying it, made the joke funny."

Edith looked at her father. "What dirty word?"

Her father cleared his throat. " 'Cunt.' In Middle English it was *cunte*, originally derived from the Latin *cunnus*, and meaning vagina. It was one of the taboo words."

"Why not simply say vagina?"

He said, "I give up. I knew very well I wasn't going to be able to explain dirty jokes. In fact, I'm not sure I understand why *I* ever thought they were funny. Good-bye. I'm off to see someone on a suggestion of Julian's that I'm not sure I understand either." He left, shaking his head.

Edith asked Julian, "Do you know any more dirty jokes?"

"No," he said definitely, sitting down across from her. He brought his notes from his side pocket.

"What do you have there?" she said.

"Some notes I was going to ask your father about, but it occurs to me that as a student of anthropology, you might be more up on it than he is. It has to do with crime."

"Crime? Oh, of course. Fascinating. I spent over a year studying it. It must have been fabulous, living back when they had crime."

He let the breath out of his lungs. "Yeah," he said. "Never a dull moment. No more crime these days, hey?"

"No. Of course not."

He didn't bother to disguise his skepticism as he

fumbled through his notes. "All right. Now let me state my case. When I went into hibernation, we had one hell of a lot of crime. It was growing so fast it was hard to keep statistics."

He looked down at his papers. "For instance, we had petty crime, such as shoplifting, avoiding paying your fare when getting on a subway or bus, children sneaking into movies, walking out on a bill in a restaurant, figuring out methods of making long distance calls on the telephone without paying." He paused. "Then there were servants pilfering about the household, servants getting a kickback from the butchershop and other stores where they purchased supplies for their employers. Trivia such as that."

"Fascinating," she repeated.

"Yeah," he muttered. "I once had a houseman who drank up three cases of vintage champagne on me." He went back to his notes. "Then we had crimes of violence. Mugging, kidnapping, piracy even, in some parts of the world, murder, rape, robbery of homes, stores, warehouses, and banks.

"And along in here we have a whole variety of odds and ends: confidence games, prostitution, gambling, blackmail, pickpocketing, smuggling, cattle rustling, extortion. Actually, the list is endless. At the very top, even more lucrative than bank robbery, and certainly more often committed, there's embezzlement."

"Yes," she said brightly. "I studied all about it. Men like Dillinger, Pretty Boy Floyd, Baby Face Nelson, Al Capone."

He looked at her sarcastically. "So no more, eh?"

She shook her head.

"No more police, no more jails. Don't need 'em any more, right?"

"That's right," she said reasonably.

He threw down the sheaf of notes on the coffee table.

"Why not? All through history we've had crime, since first some caveman slugged his neighbor over the head with a club and swiped his wife. So now, all of a sudden, why has it ended?"

"Because the reasons ended."

He took her in silently.

She said, "Now see here. All those different types of crimes you mentioned fit roughly into one of two categories; those committed for the sake of money, and those due to mental illness. Obviously, now that we've eliminated money, crimes that dealt with stealing, as such, were abolished out of hand. What would you steal, these days? Those that dealt with mental illness are now in the hands of the Medical Guild, not police, courts, and jails."

She thought about it. "Why, even in your day how did they deal with a shoplifter who was found to be a kleptomaniac?"

"Okay. But look, take a present-day embezzler. Suppose you had someone working in the part of the data banks dealing with what we would have called banking—the credit records. Someone in a position to so alter the records that he deposited to his own account, say, twice as much credit as the other citizens are granted from their Guaranteed Annual Income. What would you do with him?"

Edith sighed. "Jule, in the first place he would

have no motive for doing such a thing since he already receives all that he needs. You can't eat more than three or four meals a day, you can't wear more than one outfit of clothes at a time, and you can't sleep in more than one bed. As things are now, most people don't use up their yearly quota of credit. What in the world would you do with twice as much? But if such a thing did happen, then obviously the person involved would be mentally deranged and the Medical Guild would treat him."

"And during the time he was being treated, he would still continue to receive his Guaranteed Annual Income?"

"But of course."

Julian sighed. "Okay. All right. But how about rape? Don't tell me there are no longer crimes of passion."

"Yes, there are; seldom, but sometimes. As to rape, sex is so free, so easily available to all, that only a terribly upset person would resort to rape for sexual satisfaction. In which case, once again, it is a matter for the Medical Guild to treat the poor harassed individual."

"But suppose in committing the rape, the rapist kills the girl. Suppose the rapist is a sadist."

She looked at him in puzzlement. "But surely even in your time a sadist was given psychiatric care rather than punishment."

"Sometimes," he muttered. "Sometimes they were executed, or given life imprisonment."

"How terrible!"

"Suppose it's a crime against the State?"

"What State? There is no State. The State was an

institution for the purpose of maintaining a class-divided society. It was organized with laws, police and military, courts and prisons to maintain the status quo under slavery, feudalism, capitalism, or state-capitalism, which was what the Soviet-type communism was really all about. Today, we have no State, since we have no class or classes to be kept subjugated.''

''What I mean is, suppose someone comes along who wants to overthrow this so-called Golden Rule society of yours. What do you do with him?''

''Nothing. Any citizen is free to advocate any change.''

''But suppose he wants to overthrow the system?''

''If he could convince the majority of our citizens that his plan was appropriate, then it would be done.''

Julian was becoming impatient with her. ''But suppose he knew that he couldn't convince a majority and resorted to force and violence. In the old days, in the United States, it was theoretically legal to advocate a basic change. The country was full of minority parties and groups who wanted to establish everything from socialism to anarchy. But you had to advocate that it be accomplished by peaceful means—the ballot. When somebody came along such as the IWW, the Wobblies, or the early Communist Party, who favored armed revolt, the police, the F.B.I., and everyone else landed on them like a ton of bricks.''

The idea was so foreign to Edith that she had to think it over. She said finally, ''He'd have his work cut out trying to accomplish it. For one thing, in your day half the citizens in the country seemed to possess guns. If not, they were easily obtained, even after various laws were passed to control them. But today I would estimate that not one person in fifty owns a firearm. Hunting is no longer a popular sport; we tend to protect our wildlife. Those who do have guns usually have small-caliber ones for use in marksmanship clubs. They would hardly be suitable for armed revolt.''

"But suppose a few thousand people did arm themselves," he argued, "even with these small-caliber guns, and seized the government?"

"Jule, Jule, you know enough about the manner in which the country is run now to realize how silly that sounds. We have no government in the sense that applied in the middle of the twentieth century. The government that we do have, if that is what you want to call it, is not in control of the country. Let us suppose that you did seize all the members of the Production Congress. What would have been accomplished? They are not in control of the nation. The production of the industries and the other necessary work would go on. We would simply elect new members to a new Production Congress. But it is all so ridiculous. What would motivate such people? What would they gain that they do not have now?"

Julian grabbed up his notes and fumbled through them. "Oh, yeah," he said. "Somebody—it was you, I think—told me that narcotics were legal now. Anybody can try them."

"Yes. If you become addicted and wish to be cured, the cure is immediate and you develop a built-in allergy to the drug you were on. Both a physical and psychological allergy, so that you both don't want to ever try it again and physically are incapable of standing it."

Julian sighed. "It was one of the big problems of my time."

Edith said, "When drugs were first legalized and taken out of the hands of the criminals, they were given quite a go. Then, as with pornography in Denmark, and later in the States, particularly after an extensive educational campaign in the media, use fell off to the vanishing point. I tried smoking opium once, out of sheer curiosity."

"*You* did? You don't look the type. What happened?"

She was indignant. "But of course I'm the type. I keep telling you that I am an amateur anthropologist. Man has smoked, eaten, and drunk opium for thousands of years."

"What happened to you?"

"The first time? It made me sick."

"What do you mean, the first time? What happened the second time?"

"It wasn't so bad. I had some very nice dreams. I had read up on it, so I knew I had a good chance of becoming ill the first few times I smoked. But I went on and saw it through."

He shook his head. "It simply doesn't seem like Edith Leete. Did you finally wind up taking the cure?"

"The cure?"

"For addiction."

"Oh, Jule. Don't be ridiculous. I didn't become addicted. I simply tried it a few times and then stopped. It bored me."

Julian said, "Okay. Let's get back to crime. What I want to know is what the hell happened to the criminals when these changes of yours started taking place? What happened to the Mafia, the Syndicate, Cosa Nostra? What did you have to do, shoot them all?"

She rubbed a hand down over her face in a gesture of despair. "Jule, Jule." Then, "The average criminal in any society is not an affluent man. For every Lucky Luciano—was that his name? It's been years since I studied it."

"Yes, Lucky," Julian said. "As a matter of fact, I met him a couple of times in Naples. Well, it was Capri, actually, just off the coast. He was a rather quiet type. Quite a gentleman, in a way. But there was death behind his eyes."

"Good heavens, how wonderful," she said. "For me it's history. It's like your telling me you knew, well, Lincoln or General Grant or someone like that."

Julian said, "My family began its fortune during the Grant administration. There were many opportunities, if you had the connections."

She said, "At any rate, for every Luciano, Costello, or Capone, there were a thousand petty thieves, dope peddlers, counterfeiters, and so forth whose average take, over the years spent in crime, was less than that of a worker in industry, especially when one considers the years in prison. Let me see if I can remember his name . . . yes, Willy 'The Actor' Sutton, one of the most successful bank robbers. He once figured out that during the forty years in which he had been engaged in crime, or was imprisoned, he had averaged less than two thousand dollars a year in 'take-home pay.' Of course, deducted from his gross income were bribes to the police and crooked politicians, lawyers' fees, exorbitant prices for hideouts, and other professional expenses.''

"What's your point?''

"You asked what happened to the criminal element when our new Society of the Golden Rule emerged. Certainly, a few Godfathers of the Mafia and such well-to-do criminals opposed the new way of things as strongly as any capitalist. But the overwhelming majority of smaller fry were as much in support of the changes as their more law-abiding citizens.''

Julian slumped back, tossing his notes to the table once again.

"I don't know,'' he said. "I've been being very righteous all along here. But the fact of the matter is that when I was the head of West Enterprises, it sometimes became difficult to figure out where honesty ended and crime began. I've been hauled into court several times.''

She nodded. "Yes, I know, Jule. Remember, along with my father and mother, I have studied your life just about all my life. I probably know things about you that you don't. . . .''

He scowled at her. "What's that supposed to mean?''

She got to her feet and walked over to one of her father's bookshelves. "Father is one of the last of the book collectors. If he had his way, he'd have a thousand volumes rather than relying on the International Data Banks. Now, where in the devil is the one I want?''

He waited for her to find whatever it was she was looking for. Eventually, she returned.

"Ferdinand Lundberg," she said.

"I'll be damned. I know that name. Seems to me he was a professor at one of the big schools. He wrote a couple of muckraker books, as I recall. I don't think I read them."

"Yes," she said grimly. "You with your talk of crime, darling. Listen to this:

" 'Most offenses open to members of the upper socioeconomic class . . . were dealt with by special administrative tribunals. The offenses were mostly variants of fraud or conspiracy. When they were committed against the broad public they called for relatively light penalties, seldom prison terms. Verdicts against the offender were often carefully phrased so as to be non-stigmatic . . . Even when a member of the upper socioeconomic class was found guilty of a stigmatic crime and was about to be sentenced, there was a marked difference in the language of the judge. Often in the case of a culprit of the lower classes the judge administered a savage tongue-lashing, while the defendant hung his head and his family sobbed, terrorized. But when upper-class culprits had been convicted in criminal court of using the mails to defraud the general public, the judge . . . typically began by saying: "You are men of affairs, of experience, of refinement and culture, of excellent reputation and standing in the business and social world." They were in fact, as the judicial process had just disclosed, *criminals*. This difference in attitude of judges is often pronounced. Severely reprehensive toward members of the lower classes, the judges become wistful, melancholy, or sadly philosophical when sentencing men of the upper class. (After all, they both come from the same class, may have gone to the same school, and may belong to the same clubs.). . . . Many members of the upper classes did commit offenses for which the government held them accountable. But in most cases special arrangements had been made to handle them with kid gloves and in many cases to administer by way of punishment a slap on the wrist.' ''

Julian laughed.

Her eyes narrowed. ''What's funny?''

He rubbed a hand over his chin. ''Nothing, really. It's absolutely true. Actually, I didn't usually even appear in court. My attorneys represented me. One of the judges I remember was in college with me. We used to call him Fartface.''

''Fartface?''

''One of those taboo four-letter words your father mentioned. At any rate, he was on the take and——''

''On the take?''

''Ummm . . . that is, he was susceptible to bribery if you handled it in a careful, civilized manner.''

''How in the world did you handle bribery in a careful, civilized manner?''

He looked at her, knowing she wouldn't understand what he was going to say. ''In this particular case I gave his daughter a wedding present . . . fifty thousand dollars.'' He added absently, ''Tax free, obviously. Fifty thousand dollars from my account in Switzerland, in thousand-dollar bills.''

She was wide-eyed. ''What did you get in return?''

He considered, remembering back down over the years. "Actually, what was involved was one of the smaller countries in Central America."

Edith was incredulous. "You mean you bought a whole country?"

He said wearily, "That isn't the way it works. It's very complicated and, in fact, *I* don't know how it works. I had people who worked for me who knew how it works. That's how we all operated: Hughes, Getty, all of us. We could hire brains; we didn't have to have any."

She said, "I can't believe this."

"I gave you the wrong idea. I didn't *buy* a country. Who in the hell wants a country? You'd have to worry about schools, hospitals, all the rest of it. What I bought was . . . well, control of everything that was worth owning in the country. The right to exploit it." He added cynically, "Including the president and senate. Come to think of it, whether or not they were worth owning is moot."

She regarded him coldly and said, "I think your actions were disgusting."

He came to his feet.

"Yes, I know. Looking back on it, so do I."

Chapter Thirteen

The Year 1949

THE NIGHTMARE WAS not a new one. It was as vivid as any of the others, though not so upsetting as the war dreams.

The event which came back to him had taken place when he was about fifteen, a teenager. His parents had died in the racing crash only the year before, and his uncle, who had taken over the raising of the heir to the West Enterprises fortune, had suggested a world cruise to take his mind off the tragedy.

The luxury cruise ship had traveled east from New York, and the early weeks of the trip weren't of particular interest to the young Julian. He had been to Europe many times, many times he had sailed in the Mediterranean. However, once they passed through the Suez Canal and entered the Red Sea, he was in new territory. From Aden, at that time as British as Gibraltar, they had taken off across the Arabian Sea for Bombay, their first Indian port.

He took one of the passenger launches from the ship to the harbor landing before the Gateway to India.

He sat in the bow looking at the harbor with its myriad strange-looking craft. He had never seen lateen sails before, let alone outriggers. The vessels were a study in contrasts, ranging from such ultra-modern ships as their own Scandinavian steamer, to Arab dhows. The guide who had accompanied them from the ship to show them the city, explained that the dhows sailed all the way from Africa, during the monsoon season, and had been doing so since before the days of the Roman Empire.

Julian was one of the first off the launch. As a result, he was the first to be accosted by the beggars. There were at least a dozen of them, barefoot, ragged, dirty; the women all had at least one child, usually naked. Julian winced, being a sensitive boy at this point in his life, but he hadn't as yet changed any money and carried only traveller's checks. He had never seem a grimier lot, all thin to the point of emaciation.

He made his way through them as best he could, by looking up at the massive edifice, the Gateway of India, a Victorian arch of stone. The guide was saying that it served as a place of reception on important ceremonial occasions.

Leaving the others, Julian made his way through the arch to the large square beyond. There were more beggars here, each more ragged and dirty than the last. He looked about and spotted what appeared to be a police officer: a tall, handsome man with a thick black beard which was gathered up in a little net, and a white turban. He was in uniform and carried a swagger stick. He wore an iron-handled knife at his belt and an iron bangle on his left wrist. Julian was to find out later that the man was a Sikh.

He approached and said, "I beg your pardon. Could you direct me to the Taj Mahal Hotel?"

The other touched his turban in an easygoing salute, and pointed. "That is the Taj, right over there, sir."

It was only a few hundred yards away, and as Julian walked toward it he could see that it was a large building, undoubtedly built in the old Victorian days of the Empire. It reminded him of a Gothic British railway station. There were two turbaned men at the door. One of them opened it at Julian's approach, bowing in servile fashion.

The reception hall beyond was as one might have expected from the exterior, and Julian could have been in one of the older London hotels had it not been for the fact that all of the employees wore white turbans and had very dark complexions.

He went to the desk, receiving another servile bow, and said, "I wish to see Edward Fitz-James."

"Yes, sir. Sir Edward is not in his suite, sir. Only a few minutes ago I saw him ascend to the lounge on the second floor." The clerk indicated a large, red-carpeted stairway.

"Thank you," Julian said, evidently somewhat to the man's surprise.

He ascended the stairs and found another turbaned Indian at its head. There seemed to be a multitude of employees in this hotel.

"Could you point out Edward Fitz-James to me, please?"

The other blinked at the *please*, bowed and said, "That is Sir Edward over there at the small table near the window, *sahib*."

Sir Edward, yet. Julian hadn't known the man he

was seeking held a title. Fitz-James had once had business dealings with his father, and had become somewhat of a friend of the Wild Wests. Julian had been given an introduction by his uncle, who had evidently either written or cabled ahead, since Julian had received a radiogram arranging for a get-together.

Julian approached and asked politely, "Sir Edward Fitz-James?" The man who looked up at him stiffly was a stereotype of the bluff Britisher: possibly fifty-five, maybe thirty pounds overweight, too red in the face, with a toothbrush mustache. He wore white shorts to the knee, a white shirt, heavy walking shoes and white woolen socks almost up to the knee.

He stood up. "You must be Julian West, I wouldn't wonder. Resemble your father a bit." He put out a beefy hand to shake and said, "Do sit down, dear boy."

"Thank you, sir," Julian said, and took an over-stuffed leather chair across from the Englishman.

Sir Edward said jovially, "I say, if you walked over from the gate, you must already be bloody hot. Terrible climate here, isn't it? Do have a lime squash."

Then Julian noticed that he had a tall glass before him, well frosted, which contained a slightly greenish beverage. He turned and snapped his fingers imperiously at the nearest Indian, who hurried over.

"Another lime squash," Sir Edward commanded. "And put a move into it."

"Yes, Sir Edward," the man said and hurried away.

"Beggars are slow as turtles," the Britisher commented in a voice loud enough to carry to the man and half the other waiters in the lounge. "You have to learn the drill here. Keep the niggers in their place, don't you know?"

Julian couldn't think of anything to say to that so he kept his peace. He found the other a bit on the overwhelming side.

"Read about your father and mother," Sir Edward said. He puffed out his cheeks in what he probably thought was an expression of sympathy. "Bloody shame. Charming chap, your father. Mother a beautiful woman. One of the most vivacious women I've met, I wouldn't wonder."

"Thank you, sir. My uncle Albert said that you used to race with father, on the Riviera."

"Jolly well told. Never forget the first time I saw him. Just brought in a Jaguar, a quarter mile ahead of his nearest opponent. I thought to meself, now there's a sharp chap. Before the day was out we made friends."

Julian's lime squash had come. He lifted it up.

Sir Edward said, raising his own glass in a toast, "All the best, dear boy."

What was the British toast? "Cheers, sir." He tried the drink and found it to be possibly the best soft drink he'd ever had. It was something like lemonade, except that it had soda in it rather than water, and, of course, it was made with limes not lemons.

Sir Edward grimaced. "Could use a spot of gin. Bloody beggars have prohibition now. Damned nuisance."

Julian said carefully, almost apologetically, "If you don't like it here, sir, why do you remain?"

Sir Edward grunted his equivalent of a laugh. "No use mucking around with the answer to that, dear boy. This is where the action is, as you Yankees say. When the Indians gained their bloody independence, His Majesty's governmental officials returned to England, don't you know? But we British business-men didn't. We stayed on. In fact, there are more English in India today than during the days of the Raj."

He looked at his watch. "But, I say, suppose we mosey along and see a bit of the town? Bit interesting for you, I wouldn't wonder. First trip to India and all that rot."

They left the hotel and started up Colaba Road. Even in this Europeanized area, Julian couldn't help but note the teeming multitudes of Indians. He had never seen such diversity of colorful costume.

"Bloody mess of the bounders, eh?" the Eng-lishman said. "Pushing half a billion in all. More than four million in Bombay alone, I shouldn't won-der. Jolly well too many of them. I'd jolly well like to go through the countryside and sterilize every other male, don't you know?"

Julian said, "I don't think I've ever seen anything so crowded except Times Square on New Year's Eve."

They had turned up Mahatma Gandhi Road.

"Son of a bitch, as you Yankees say," Sir Edward commented about Gandhi. "Caused us ever so much trouble, but I suppose you can't hold it against a chap for trying to get his own way, now can you?"

"I suppose not," Julian said. "They certainly do

have a great many different styles of clothes, don't they?"

The Englishman turned guide. "Way you can tell the bloody bounders apart," he said. "See that one over there? The better dressed one? That's a Brahman." He sneered. "The nigger equivalent of an aristocrat. They wear a sacred thread over one shoulder and have a mark of one of the Hindu gods chalked on their forehead, rising from the bridge of the nose like two thin white horns. That's one of the marks of Vishnu, the Preserver. Ridiculous, isn't it?"

"What kind is that one?"

"Moslem. You can usually tell them from a Hindu because they wear a black fur cap. She's a Moslem too. They wear that enveloping *chadar* or *burqa*. Looks like an animated tent, don't you think?"

Most of the women, other than the occasional European, wore what Julian knew was called a sari, but there were a double score of styles.

"That's a Bengali," Sir Edward said. "He's wearing what they call the *dhoti*. All-purpose white garment. Sometimes it hangs almost to the ground like a sarong, or sometimes they tuck it up like that chap, like a loincloth. Sometimes the bounders wear a waistcoat with it, sometimes a shirt with the tails flopping outside. Silly-looking bunch of monkeys, don't you think?"

A girl whom Julian would have thought no more than ten years of age came alongside and clawed at his arm. In spite of her age, she was carrying a baby. She was grubby, barefoot, and wore a single dirty rag.

181

She whined, "No mama, no papa. Hungry, hungry, hungry. Money, money, money."

Julian stared at her, even as they continued to walk.

"Ignore the bloody little bitch," Sir Edward commanded.

"But she looks like she's half starving," Julian said.

"Jolly well be better if she did, you know. Professional. Whole caste of them here in India. Parents were beggars, grandparents, all the way back to the days of Alexander the Great or whoever, don't you know? See that baby? She probably rented it this morning."

The child was still tagging along with her burden. "No mama, no papa . . ." Julian was embarrassed, and looked out of the side of his eyes to see how the passersby were taking the scene.

"Rented it?" he said.

"Why, yes. And sometimes beggar parents take their children and maim them. Twist their legs or arms around, blind them, or whatever, to gain sympathy. Bloody heathens."

Julian felt slightly nauseated at the idea. He had changed a twenty-dollar traveler's check at the hotel, and now had a pocketful of rupees and naye paise. He had gotten nearly five rupees to the dollar, to the Englishman's disgust, and had been informed that on the black market, which Sir Edward offered to direct him to, he could have gotten half again as much. Julian had told him that it wasn't important.

But, at any rate, he was now in a position to give the ten-year-old a coin or so.

Sir Edward snickered. "You think she is starving?

Look at that gold ring in her ear. She's a professional beggar, specializing in we whites. Some of the other beggars specialize in pilgrims and hang around the temples. Supposedly, the pilgrims gain merit in the eyes of the gods by giving to them. And they usually give one naye paise, about one twentieth of one of your Yankee cents."

The child beggar followed them at least three or four blocks. In spite of his embarrassment, Julian continued to ignore her. After she dropped away, back into the teeming mob of pedestrians, another beggar, an unbelievably old man, took up the pursuit, whining in some language Julian had never heard before.

The Englishman snorted cynically. "That's the end of her beat, dear boy. If she continued to follow us, the others would give her a bit of a show at the end of the day. Do you know what would happen if you gave this bloody nigger something?"

Julian said, "Well, no, but he seems to be very old."

"He'd pass the information along, don't you know, to his, ah, colleagues. Within ten minutes, you'd have half a dozen of the blighters trailing you."

Before them reared an enormous Indian building, as large as a cathedral. It must have cost millions, Julian decided, but somehow, for him, it lacked beauty in a country so rich in beggars.

"Mumbadevi Temple," his guide said. "The town's jolly well overrun with temples. Hindu temples, Moslem temples, Zoroastrian, Buddhist, Jainian. . . . I dare say there are hundreds in all. The Zoroastrians have an interesting bit. They don't believe in either burial or cremation. Up in the Hanging

Gardens they have several of what they call Towers of Silence. When one of them dies, his body is put on the top of one of the towers and buzzards come and eat the corpse. After a week or so of exposure, the bones are taken down and thrown into the tower's well. Bloody gruesome, eh? You can watch the buzzards at work from a nearby hill.''

Julian's nausea was not diminishing. "I . . . I don't think I'd like that.''

He looked at the ornate, towering temple.

A cadaverously thin, barefooted, ragged man who seemingly was about to enter the temple gate suddenly staggered, his eyes popping in horror. Blood gushed from his mouth, spewing out onto the sidewalk. He staggered again, fell forward onto his face.

Julian automatically started forward.

Sir Edward quickly took his arm. "He's beyond help, dear boy. Probably dead by now. The meat wagon will undoubtedly be along shortly. Besides, how would you like to catch whatever he had?''

The other pedestrians walked around the fallen man, ignoring him.

"Meat wagon?'' Julian repeated, unable to keep his eyes from the body. He had never seen a person die before. It was all he could do to keep from vomiting.

Sir Edward hurried him on. "Every night, several hundred of the street people die. City trucks come around and pick up the bodies, don't you know?'' He added musingly, "Fewer seem to die during the day hours, but you see the corpses around from time to time.''

"Street people?"

"I dare say there are some half a million niggers here in Bombay that have no homes. They live on the streets, sleep on the streets at night. There are more than six-hundred thousand in Calcutta."

The boy was appalled. "Can't the government do something about them?"

"Dear boy, between a third and a half of the population of India goes to bed hungry every night. Probably some fifty million are starving to death, at a greater or slower pace. What would you expect the government to do? It's deeply in debt as it is. My own concern is selling them tanks and armored cars, and most of it has to go on the cuff, as you Yankees call it."

The Britisher indicated a smaller street. "We can cut through here to the Crawford Market. Largest in town, I wouldn't wonder. What do the tourist ads always say? Picturesque and all that rot."

They were in little more than an alley with tiny shacks on each side. Colored saris hung from some of the windows to dry and a few of the dwellings had plants suspended from the walls in old tin cans.

Halfway down the alley, Julian came to a halt. In a broken wheelbarrow were two tiny children, breathing heavily, their eyes very round. Both were naked, with arms and legs so thin as to be not much thicker than a piece of chalk; both had bellies swollen up to the size of watermelons.

He looked wildly at his companion, "Have they been abandoned by their parents?"

The other took him by the arm to lead him on. "Possibly. Come, there's nothing you can do."

Julian pulled away. "We can take them . . . take them to a hospital. See they're fed. Have a doctor——"

Sir Edward said impatiently, "I told you there were some fifty million starving in India at any one time. You could drop the whole West fortune into this bottomless pit, and it wouldn't have any noticeable effect whatsoever."

He took Julian by the arm again and led him to the end of the alleyway and the wider street beyond.

Julian wrenched his arm away once more. "I . . . I don't want to see any more. I want to go back to the ship."

The other was miffed. He looked at his watch. "Very well. I had planned to take you to lunch. Charming restaurant called The Other Room, at the Ambassador Hotel, don't you know? European cuisine, none of this bloody nigger stuff."

The boy looked at him. "How many of these Indians could eat on what it would cost us there for a single meal?"

The other laughed his short, humorless laugh. "Hundreds of them, I shouldn't wonder. Dear boy, the average Indian doesn't spend in a year what it would cost us to lunch at The Other Room."

Julian shook his head. "I'm going back to the ship."

"Very well. No point in mucking around. Just head down this street. You'll come out on the Frere Road. Turn right for about a mile and you'll come to the Old Customs House and the government dockyard. You'll be able to rent a boat there to return you to the cruise ship, I wouldn't wonder." Sir Edward was obviously mildly irritated.

Julian extended his hand. "Thank you very much, sir."

"Oh, I say, not at all, dear boy. Give my regards to your uncle when the trip is over."

Although the directions had seemed very simple, Julian managed to lose his way. After a time, he found himself in a slum street, not much different than the alleyway in which he had seen the starving children.

From a dark doorway a voice hissed at him, "Sahib?"

He came to a halt, frowning. He could make out an Indian woman in a pink sari, a caste mark on her forehead. She had by the hand a child of possibly four or five, with its own small sari. It was a beautiful child.

Julian came closer and said, "Yes?"

The woman beckoned to him, but he still didn't understand. "What do you want?" he asked.

She reached down and lifted the child's sari.

Julian blanched. At this point in his life, he had never had sexual relations, but there was no misunderstanding the gesture. He was being offered the child's body. The woman was attempting to sell the little girl sexually. Her own daughter? Probably, he thought numbly.

It was at this point that he awoke, the horror still with him.

As he lay there, the rest of the experience came back. He had returned to the ship, after getting directions from another Sikh police officer, and had remained on it for the balance of the stay in India. He had not gone ashore again until they reached Hong Kong, and then only to take an airplane back to the States.

Spending the whole West fortune would not have been a drop in the bottomless pit of India's poverty, according to Sir Edward Fitz-James. But when he had finally come into his inheritance, couldn't he have done *something*, maybe set up a foundation to at least help out? Perhaps some hospitals, or orphanages?

But no, he told himself now, he hadn't done a thing. Like his fellows, he had looked at philanthropy largely as a tax dodge. Born to wealth, he had been contemptuous of those who didn't have it; it was a God-given privilege that he enjoyed because of his innate right to enjoy it. The only foundations West Enterprises had ever endowed had in one manner or another profited him, including the one set up for Dr. Pillsbury in return for putting him into stasis.

But the poverty of India had distressed him as a boy. Looking backward now, he couldn't dismiss the poverty pockets in his own supposedly wealthy country. He had seen slums in Washington, D.C. not half a mile from the White House that were nearly as bad as those of Bombay. He had seen slums in New York, Chicago, and Los Angeles, possibly the three richest cities of the time, that were unbelievable.

Chapter Fourteen

The Year 2, New Calendar

In the past, man had little power over either his environment or his own nature. Nothing we did could fundamentally affect these factors, which were the result of natural processes that have acted over billions of years. But advances in our scientific knowledge, and the technological capabilities flowing from this knowledge, are making it possible for the human race to influence itself and its environment in major ways. . .

If the decisions are not made rationally, it is highly unlikely that we or our descendants will appreciate the world that emerges.

—Gerald Feinberg, *The Prometheus Project*

JULIAN HAD PLANNED to spend a few hours at his studies before going over to the Leetes', but it didn't work out that way.

He had hardly finished his toilet and breakfast and sat down at his desk, when the phone screen buzzed.

He activated it and was confronted with the youthful, open face of Sean O'Callahan.

"Good morning, Mr. West. I hope I'm not bothering you."

"Make it Julian. No, of course not. What can I do for you, Sean?"

He grinned. "Well, as a matter of fact, I have somewhat of a surprise for you. Can you come over to my place? I'm in Building Two, sixteenth floor, apartment sixteen-B."

"A surprise?" Julian echoed—surprised.

"That's right."

He said, "All right, I'll be right over."

"Fine." The other's face faded from the screen.

Julian stood up and made his way toward the door. He couldn't think of any particular reason to notify the Leetes of his little expedition into the outside world. In fact, unless he was mistaken, this was one of Edith's work days and hadn't Mrs. Leete said something about attending a meeting?

He took the elevator down to the metro level, and looked around. Always before when he had ventured out, one or more of the Leetes had been along, so he hadn't had to figure out the transport system.

He asked the first passerby in halting Interlingua how to get to Building Two, which he assumed to be one of the other high-rise apartment buildings in the university city. The directions were simplicity itself, and he took the next car heading for his destination.

He'd hardly had time to seat himself before they were at a new station whose sign read BUILDING TWO. He got out and made his way over to the elevator banks. From time to time people passing would smile at him in friendly fashion, and twice people nodded and said, "Mr. West," by way of greeting. Although he knew none of them, evidently his face was recognized widely. So, he was rapidly becoming a minor celebrity in spite of Dr. Leete's attempts to shield him in these early weeks of his arrival from the past.

He said, "Sixteenth Floor," into the elevator's screen and the robotlike voice answered, "Yes, Mr. West." He wondered vaguely what would happen if he went out to some place on the Pacific coast: would the elevator screens recognize him there? Were the data banks and the face of every resident of United America tied in with every screen in the country? The magnitude of it all rather boggled his mind.

There were signs on the wall on the sixteenth floor, giving directions. He had no difficulty finding Sean O'Callahan's apartment. He pressed the button, standing before the identity screen.

The door opened, and he was greeted by a beaming Sean.

"Come in and meet your surprise."

Frowning in puzzlement, Julian followed his host into the living room. Four men were seated there, including William Harrison and Frederic Ley. The other two were strangers: a young man of possibly thirty, tall, intelligent-looking, with a somewhat quizzical expression; the other must have been somewhere in his early seventies, slightly heavy, gray hair and mustache, slightly florid face.

The latter said in a slow voice, "Hello, Jule. It's been a long time."

Julian stared at him, shot a puzzled look at the

grinning Sean, then gazed back at the elderly man.

"You look exactly like you did the last time we saw each other in the Knickerbocker-Links Club in New York. I'm afraid you can't say the same about me."

"I'll be damned!" Julian exclaimed. "Bert Melville!"

"That's right, Jule. I thought you were committing suicide when you let that crackpot Doctor Pillsbury put you into hibernation; evidently he wasn't as big a crackpot as everybody thought. Here you are, looking about thirty-five. Here I am looking seventy-three and feeling every year of it. I should have let him put *me* under too."

"To wake up in a world like this?" Harrison said bitterly.

Sean led Julian over to the younger man, who stood at their approach. "This is Dave Woolman," he said, "who has one of the most fascinating jobs in the country."

Dave had a very sincere, unhumorous smile, and shook hands strongly. "I've been looking forward to meeting you. Somebody out of the past. Somebody who knew the *real* world."

Julian didn't quite get that. He said, "Nice to meet you. What's the most fascinating job in the country?"

"Sit down. Sit down, everybody," said Sean. When they were seated, he explained, "Possibly not for Dave. It's probably just tedious routine for him, but he's in charge of the Radio Astronomy Observatory on Luna."

Julian shook his head. "What's radio astronomy? Astronomy is a field on which I was completely blank even in the 1960s. You can imagine to what extent I'm ignorant now, after a third of a century of progress. Did you say Luna? You mean there's an observatory on the moon?"

Dave Woolman nodded. "It was decided as far back as 1960 that the radio telescope, rather than the spaceship, would probably be the first instrument to establish contact with intelligent life beyond the solar system. Since your time, we have receivers of such sensitivity and antennas of such enormous size, that we are optimistic about sending and picking up radio signals from the nearer stars. The search for these signals began in 1960 at the National Radio Astronomy Observatory in Greenbank, West Virginia. The Luna Observatory is a great advantage. It's located on the far side, and hence cut off from a great deal of the local radio interference that an earthbound observatory suffers."

"I'm impressed," Julian said. "Have you been able to pick up any messages from other worlds?"

A strange silence fell over the whole group.

Woolman said finally, "I am afraid I'm not in a position to answer that."

The elderly Bert Melville changed the subject. He had been looking at Julian intently, and now he turned to Harrison and said, "You know, Jule and I used to belong to a consorium based in New York, the Bahamas, and Switzerland. We used to swing some pretty big deals." His laugh quavered a bit. "Those were the days, eh, Jule? Remember the time we squeezed out Bob Percy and took over Diversified?"

"Yes. Yes, I remember that operation. Bob shot himself afterwards."

"I'd forgotten about that part of it," Melville said.

Harrison seemed slightly impatient. He said to Julian, "Did you think over what we were discussing the other day—in short, Utopias?"

"Yes, yes I did. Frankly, I didn't come up with much in the way of a conclusion."

Harrison nodded. "I was just giving you some preliminaries to work on, Mr. West. Are you acquainted with the work of a contemporary of yours, the British writer Arthur C. Clarke?"

Julian frowned a little. "It seems to me that the Leetes have mentioned him a couple of times, as a popularizer of science."

"Yes." Harrison got to his feet and went over to the library booster, which sat on the desk. He dialed as he said over his shoulder, "This is from one of his books. Astonishingly prophetic. I'll read you just this one passage.

" 'Civilization cannot exist without new frontiers; it needs them both physically and spiritually. The physical need is obvious—new lands, new resources, new materials. The spiritual need is less apparent, but in the long run it is more important. We do not live by bread alone; we need adventure, variety, novelty, romance. As the psychologists have shown by their sensory deprivation experiments, a man goes swiftly mad if he is isolated in a silent, darkened room, cut off completely from the external world. What is true of individuals is also true of societies; they too can become insane without sufficient stimulus.' "

Harrison deactivated the screen and turned back to Julian. "What's your reaction to that?"

"I don't know." Julian shifted in his chair. "It makes a lot of sense."

The seventy-three-year-old Bert Melville leaned forward impatiently. "Jule, the damn country is turning to mush. Ninety-eight percent do nothing but putter around with their hobbies: they paint paintings nobody wants to look at; they write books nobody reads; they move into mobile towns and travel around the country doing nothing but trying to enjoy themselves."

Harrison took it up with his usual energy. "Ethically, the country is going to pot. Institutions that have come down to us through the ages are being completely eroded. Look at sex. All the young people now behave like rabbits. They start educating them on how to screw in God only knows how many different positions as soon as they're into their teens. The family is disappearing, and the population is beginning to decrease. Whatever happened to religious training? The churches are empty except for old folks—those churches that remain at all."

The usually taciturn Ley put in his word. "It's like Mr. Melville said. 'The country's turning to mush.' They don't even have boxing any more. 'Somebody might get hurt.' Hell, when I was a kid Joe Louis was still alive. Fought his way up out of the slums, thrilled millions, and made millions. What's wrong with that? Give the kids a desire to make something of themselves, to fight their way up. I read about this Manolete, the bullfighter in Spain. Another slum kid, but with guts. Became the best bullfighter of all time. Made tons of bucks thrilling people, taking his chances. Inspired other poor Spanish kids to make their play for the big time. How about car racing? I was at Indianapolis one year, at the Old Brickyard. Talk about thrills. The crowd was on its feet half the time, yelling themselves crazy. Those guys that drove those cars had guts, and they inspired younger people to get in there and fight.''

''All the old virtues are topsy-turvy,'' Sean muttered. ''For instance, anybody at all can dial as much pornography as he wants from the International Data Banks. You should see some of it. A six-year-old kid can look at it if he wants.''

Julian was looking thoughtful. ''I've argued some of this with Academician Leete and his family. What he points out is that with this new system of the International Data Banks, it's the best people, those with the highest Aptitude Quotient, who wind up running the country. The rest aren't needed.''

''Ah?'' Harrison said triumphantly. ''Who says they're the best? A bunch of machines! There are some things, Mr. West, a machine can't measure.''

''The whole idea rather turned me off at the beginning,'' Julian admitted. ''But Academician Leete has some strong arguments and I don't have much material to base my disagreements on. Whom can't the computers measure?''

Harrison, in his enthusiasm, was on his feet. ''Whom can't they measure? The men who count most. The men who have counted most down through the centuries. Men with the dream, with the urge for power, with ruthless ambition, men of aggression, of charisma. The men whose ambition is such that the whole world is pushed forward as a result of their efforts.''

"Such as whom?" Julian said, his voice skeptical.

Harrison nodded at the validity of the question. "Do you know that Alexander the Great was the despair of his tutors, that Winston Churchill was a third-rater in school, that Ulysses S. Grant graduated twenty-first in a class of thirty-nine at West Point? Hitler was a high school dropout and failed his entrance examination to the art academy. Charlemagne couldn't read or write. Caesar wrote Latin inadequately, much to the embarrassment of Latin teachers to this day. Lord Nelson received only a summary education and at the age of twelve went to sea as a midshipman. Lincoln had less than a year's schooling. Washington had little formal learning; his biographer says, 'His chief education was received from practical men and outdoor occupations, not from books.' Thomas Edison had exactly three months of education and at the age of twelve became a newsboy on the railroads. Dickens had a vocabulary of twenty-five hundred words, and Shakespeare was spurned by most of the literati of his day because he never went to university.

"I could go on and on. Tell me, Mr. West, do you imagine for a moment that any of these men would be selected at Muster Day for even the meanest of positions in the present so-called Republic of the Golden Rule?"

The other men laughed scornfully.

Julian said slowly, "No. From what I understand about the computers and the Aptitude Quotient, I suppose none of them would be selected." He thought a moment. "I suppose the same thing applies to women. No reason why not."

Dave Woolman said, "Catherine the Great of Russia, one of the most famous women of all time, couldn't sign her name until she became Empress when she was past the age of forty."

Julian was listening intently.

Bert Melville spoke now. "Look at yourself, Jule. One of the most successful young men I've ever met. You doubled the fortune your father left you before you were thirty. In the Asian war, you went in as a shavetail lieutenant, though God knows you could have pulled strings in Washington. But you came out a major with a fist full of medals. When you found out you were a sick man you had the guts to undertake a dangerous experiment. Not one person in a thousand at the time thought you'd come through."

"What will happen to you under this society, Mr. West?" Harrison urged.

Julian slumped in his seat. "After I've learned the language and studied up a bit, I'll leave Leete's tutelage and be off on my own. My Aptitude Quotient will obviously not be such that I will be selected on Muster Day for a job—any job. One of the Leetes suggested that I might give some talks to the younger people, explaining day by day life in the old times before I went into stasis."

The aged Bert Melville snorted in deprecation. "Not much of a life for a man of your guts and ambition, Jule."

Julian growled at him, "So, what's the alternative? The fact of the matter is I understand that the man in the street likes what he's getting. He's secure, living the life of Riley. Here we are, five men sitting around beefing that the race has lost its dynamite, that wishy-washy people without the dream but with the ability to run up high Aptitude Quotients are at the country's helm. What can five men do?"

Once again there was silence, and once again it was Harrison who finally spoke up. "There are more of us than five, Julian."

"You mean you've got an organization?"

"Yes, of course. Nationally. And potentially a much larger one."

"Recruited from where, and from what elements?"

Bert Melville grunted at that. "There were a few billionaires and several thousand millionaires when this change took place, Jule; they and their families. There were also hundreds of thousands of Americans who felt they were on their way up, men and women on the make, as we used to call it; all these and their families."

"You can't figure on all of them."

"No, of course not. But wouldn't you have fought the change, had you been awake at the time it took place?"

"Undoubtedly," Julian answered. "Who else?"

Sean O'Callahan said, "There were a few thousand military, general and admiral rank, when the phasing out of the army, navy, and air corps took place. Not to mention tens of thousands of majors, lieutenant-colonels, and their equivalent ranks in navy and air force. Anybody who selects the military as his career sees it as a lifetime job. Practically none of these people were selected by the computers for positions in the new society."

"Who else?"

"There were other fields that almost completely disappeared," Dave Woolman said seriously. "The professionally religious, for instance. Priests, nuns, ministers, rabbis, preachers, evangelists, missionaries. A large number of them were in despair when they saw religion withering away."

"I can imagine," Julian said. "Who else doesn't like the present way?"

Harrison said somewhat impatiently, "Can't you see how many people there must be who can't adapt to this fast-changing world? Conservatives: those who liked the old ways; those who dragged their feet at the changes that applied to almost every aspect of our way of life. Suppose you were a mediumly successful farmer in Mississippi or Idaho. Your grandfather had settled your land, your father had improved it, you were born and raised on it. One day the representatives of the Republic of the Golden Rule come along and tell you that your method of farming is out—antiquated or whatever. That all farmland is being amalgamated so that it can be turned over to the latest automated farm machinery, operated largely by computers. How would you feel?"

Sean said, "All these are potential followers of ours when the break comes."

Julian eyed him. "What break?" Those they had mentioned coincided with the malcontents Edith and her father had named.

Harrison said, his voice smooth, "We can hardly tell you that, Julian, until we know that you're completely with us."

"I see. Of what use could I be to you? I'm out of my depth in this world. I don't know the ropes. I can't even speak the language very well as yet."

Sean said, "Jule, you're the type we don't have much of any more. You're a combat man, an aggressive, ambitious, tough fighter."

"I've seen combat," Fredric Ley grumbled.

Sean looked at him. "Over a third of a century ago. Jule was in combat, killing men, winning medals, a few months ago." He turned back to Julian. "We need your type. You're the leader material we need so badly. You don't have to know how to program a computer, or pilot a spaceship. We can locate lots of people to do that."

"I see. Well, what happens now?"

Harrison said, "We don't expect an immediate decision, Julian. Think about it and let us know. You can always get in touch with the organization through Sean, here."

Julian stood up. "All right, I'll think it over. Good morning, gentlemen." He looked at Bert Melville. "A real surprise to see you again, Bert."

"Oh, we'll see a good deal of each other in the future, Jule. Talk over the old days, when men were men." He blinked watery eyes in anticipation.

Sean saw Julian to the door and gave him a pat on the shoulder as he left.

Julian walked down the corridors to the elevators.

Fredric Ley packed a gun in a shoulder holster under his left arm. Supposedly it was in a hideaway rig, but Julian West had seen too many guns in his day to be fooled. There had even been times when his financial activities were such that he had retained a bodyguard, armed in much the same manner as was Ley.

Chapter Fifteen

The Year 2, New Calendar

*We look beyond the current shock front to a
wealthy and powerful and coordinated world
society . . . a society that might find out how to
keep itself alive and evolving for thousands or
millions of years. . . . It is a tremendous prospect. It is a quantum jump . . . the world is now
too dangerous for anything less than Utopia.*
                              —John R. Platt,
                          Professor of Biophysics
                              The Step to Man

JULIAN RETURNED TO his own quarters. Since he
had been revived, such a short time ago things had
been piling up. And now some of them were coming
to a head. He was being faced with various decisions,
and was inadequately prepared to make them. The
situation irritated him.

He paused before the door to his apartment, then
turned and went down to that of the Leetes. As
always, since his face was programmed into the identity screen, the door opened at his approach.

He entered the living room to find only Dr. Leete, who had a battered-looking book in his hand and an old-fashioned pencil. He was marking a passage.

"Good morning," he said. "Edith and Martha are both out. I called you an hour or so ago, and you seemed to have left too."

Julian nodded. "Have you made any progress with that suggestion of mine yesterday?"

Leete chuckled with self-approval and reached into an inner pocket to emerge with a device that looked like an old fountain pen.

"Yes, and——"

Julian put his finger to his lips in the age-old gesture for silence, and motioned with his thumb to one of the bathrooms.

The other blinked, but held his peace and followed.

Inside, Julian closed the door and once again turned on the running water.

He whispered, "It certainly didn't take you long."

Leete beamed. "I ran into a bit of luck. I have a friend who putters around with electronics, physicist chap now retired, but he himself was hesitant. He had no doubt that he could eventually come up with what you wished, but had never done anything along those lines before, and he would have had to start from scratch. However, by sheer chance he has a fellow electronics buff who is fascinated by the subject of bugging and detecting bugs as it applied in your day. My friend introduced me, and Dr. Browning was absolutely delighted to find someone who would even listen to details of his various projects. He had a score and more of some of the most complicated gadgets you ever saw. Did you know that it is possible to pick up from half a mile away the conversation of someone driving along in a vehicle?''

Julian raised a hand to cut him off. ''Yes, I've heard about it. But I don't believe we'll be dealing with anything that sophisticated. What's that he gave you?''

''He said that it was possibly the most universal, uh, *mop* he had on hand. But he said that if it didn't work to come back and——''

''Did you tell him what you wanted it for?''

The doctor looked at him blankly. ''I don't *know* what we want it for.''

''Did he show you how to operate it?''

''Oh, it's simplicity itself. He demonstrated it in his workshop. Those little bugs of his are simply fascinating. He had my friend and me hide several of them about the shop while he was out of the room and then——''

''But how do you operate it?''

''You simply press this button on the end and direct the other end at any place you think a bug might be. If there is one, it buzzes.''

''All right. Now keep mum.''

Julian turned off the water and led the way back to the living room, followed by his mystified host. Leete sat down and stared after him as he toured the room, pointing the electronic mop here, there, everywhere. Finally, he approached a painting, an abstract beloved by Edith but which he thought a horror.

A faint buzz emanated from the penlike device he held in his hand.

Academician Raymond Leete's eyes grew huge.

Julian came closer. The buzz intensified. He deactivated the mop and stuck it in the breast pocket of his jerkin, and reached up and removed the painting from the wall. Silently, he pointed at the circular little device stuck there. It was colored the same as the wall itself and was not easy to detect.

Then Julian put the painting back in place and resumed his search of the room.

He said conversationally, "You know, when we were talking about the socioeconomic changes I was continually surprised at how quickly it all got rolling, once it started moving at all, and how far it went. I would have thought it would take at least a century to have evolved to this point."

He continued to search the walls, but without further luck.

Leete was far from stupid, and he followed Julian's lead.

"It's in the nature of such movements to get out of hand, Jule; to move faster than the 'leaders' expected. Take the French Revolution, or the American Revolution of 1776, for that matter. Or the Russian Mensheviks, who started the revolt against the Czar expecting to set up a Western-style parliamentary government, but soon had matters taken out of their hands by the rampaging Bolsheviks. So it was in this country too. When the Second Constitutional Convention met, even those most active in the beginning had no idea how far it would go. Many who started as leaders dropped out hopelessly conservative before it was through."

There seemed to have been only the one bug in the living room. Julian gestured for the other to follow him and went into the kitchen, complete with its little breakfast nook where the Leetes usually ate. The bug was more easily detected here. It was under the table, once again neatly camouflaged.

Julian kept up a running chatter as they went from room to room.

He said, "Something Edith said the other day has come back to me. She spoke of the Soviet system as being state-capitalism; they called it communism."

Leete went along with him, his eyes still wide in disbelief. "Remember the old story of Lincoln? He said to a visiting delegation, 'If you called a sheep's tail a leg, how many legs would the sheep have?' And someone answered, 'Five'. And Lincoln said, 'No, the sheep would have four legs. Calling a tail a leg doesn't make it one.' "

Julian laughed. "So?"

"So when the bureaucracy running the Soviet complex called itself communist, or socialist, it wasn't necessarily either system. In your day, the Soviet Union paid lip service to socialism but exploited wage labor, had money, banks, and most of the other symptoms of a capitalist society. The only difference was that the production and distribution system was not owned by individual capitalists; they were owned by the State. And the State was owned by the Communist Party, the leaders of which, at least, led the same good life as did the capitalists in the West. To a lesser extent the same thing applied to, say, Sweden and Great Britain, both of whom paid lip service to socialism—one of the most elastic terms ever to come into the socioeconomic lexicon. As capitalism develops, it becomes less and less practical for some basic industries to remain in private hands, and less profitable. For instance, take the post office. In the early days in America, it was in the hands of private enterprise—even up until the days of Wells Fargo and the Pony Express. But an industrialized, modern society must have an efficient, integrated postal system. A businessman in early New York who wanted to get an important letter to San Francisco had to send it half a dozen times by half a dozen routes and pray one got through. It wasn't very efficient. The same thing applied in many countries to railroads; they were inefficient in private hands so they nationalized them. In England the coal mines didn't allow for a profit so the mines were nationalized and took a loss on production, piously calling it socialism. The miners, of course, were as exploited as they had been under private ownership."

They checked out every room in the Leete quarters. They located bugs in the living room, the kitchenette, the dining room, in the bedroom of Martha and Raymond Leete, and in his study. There were none in Edith's room, nor any in the baths or the hallway.

When they were done, they returned to the living room. Academician Leete's face was set in an expression of absolute astonishment.

Julian said, keeping his voice level, "Oh, by the way, I have something in my apartment I want very much to show you. Have you time to drop by?"

"Of course, Julian."

On the way down the hall, Leete whispered, "Can we talk out here?"

"I would think so, but I'm not sure. Hold it for awhile."

In the West apartment, they went through the same routine. In the living room, even as he began to explore with the mop, Julian said, "Can I get you a drink?"

"Why, I wouldn't mind a glass of Moselle."

"I think I'll have my usual Scotch and soda. Here, I'll dial them."

He pointed at the auto-bar and while Leete went through the routine of getting their drinks, Julian continued mopping his quarters.

As he searched, he kept up the former trend of their conversation. "What would you say the present socioeconomic system could be called?"

Leete waited a moment, as though considering the question. "Actually," he said, "I rebel against labels—capitalism, feudalism, socialism, communism, liberalism, technocracy." He snorted in deprecation. "I even rebel against the use of our back-patting term Republic of the Golden Rule. It's all a great deal of nonsense. Society is in a continual state of flux. Under the chattel slavery system of Greece, and later on, you had a certain amount of feudalism, and you even had an emerging capitalist class. What do we have today? Once again, I rebel against labels, but I suppose if you must have terminology, I would say . . ." he hesitated, ". . . well, I would say we have somewhat of a combination of syndicalism, socialism—the DeLeonist type—technocracy, and meritocracy, as that brilliant Englishman Michael Young called it."

Julian's mop began to buzz. He traced it down. The

bug was neatly located immediately below his phone screen, right on his desk.

He said, "Meritocracy? That's a new one for me. It must have come along after I went into hibernation."

He went on into his bedroom, and Leete, now completely aware of the game though not quite understanding it, continued to talk.

"I'm not sure when he wrote his book. I think it was entitled *The Rise of the Meritocracy*. You can look it up at your leisure in the International Data Banks. He foresaw something like our present Aptitude Quotient. I think his formula was I.Q. plus effort equals merit. As I recall, he projected himself into the year 2034 A.D. His basic idea was that even in his day it was no longer enough to be somebody's nephew to obtain a reasonable post in society. Under Meritocracy, experts in education and selection apply scientific principles to sift out the leaders. In a word, you must show 'merit.' Then he asks the question, is this an undivided blessing?"

Julian had returned to the living room after completely exploring his apartment. He went over to his desk and upended the phone screen. Then he took his small pocket knife out and regarded the bug for a long quizzical moment. He opened the knife and carefully pried the listening device off—it had been held onto the surface by a suction cup—and examined it carefully.

In his time, in the cutthroat field of international finance, Julian West had often had his phones tapped, his quarters bugged, and, in turn had done the same to his rivals. However, he himself was not up on the mechanics of the thing. There were experts to be hired for such matters, private detectives and such. He had long had, on full-time retainer, two former C.I.A. men.

There were two tiny screws on the surface. Using the small blade of the knife, he carefully unscrewed them, while his companion continued to watch him. The top came off and inside was a wonder of miniaturization which he understood not at all. He thought about it for awhile, deciding finally that almost anything he did would destroy its effectiveness. But that wasn't all that he wanted; when somebody came to check out why the bug had become inoperative, he didn't want it to appear as though it had been tampered with. With a shrug he inserted the small blade of the knife under a tiny disk and pried it free.

Then he put the top on the bug and screwed the tiny screws back into place. He returned the device to its exact original position, and then replaced the phone screen.

He turned to Dr. Leete. "All right, there was only the one bug in my place. I've bollixed it: we can talk."

"Should we return to my apartment and do the same to those?"

Julian shook his head. "Whoever is monitoring your apartment—and mine—would be irritated, but not surprised, if one of the bugs became inoperative. The things are delicate. But if all of them suddenly failed to transmit, then they'd know they'd been discovered and would figure out some new method of tapping you—tapping us. Leave the bugs in your apartment, warn Martha and Edith about them, and simply watch what you say."

The other was completely out of his depth. "But who would care what any of us say?"

Julian sighed. "I suspect you know. Or, at least, I suspect that you suspect. The other day, after you'd had your two run-ins with the young hoodlums, Edith suggested you get in touch with Security and report the incidents. But you clammed up. Why?"

Leete was irritated. He said, finally, "Julian, though you have been literally cramming new information ever since we revived you, there are still a million-fold matters you do not understand."

Julian was not above impatience himself. "As I am fully aware of, Raymond; however, there are some fields in which you people today are babes in the woods compared to me. Now, who are the people down enough on you to bug your apartment and attack you physically?"

Leete sighed. "Julian, for about a month now we've been telling you that this is no Utopia. There is no such thing as Utopia. Society is in a continual condition of flux. Changes have been made, are being made, and will be made."

"Okay. So what are the changes that you are actively advocating that so irritate some other elements that they're out to get you?"

"That isn't the way I would put it."

"That's the way I put it," Julian said emphatically. "Though in full realization that the world has manifold times as much knowhow as it did when I was put to sleep, I suspect that it has lost some of the knowhow of my day, that it has atrophied away."

The academician sighed again. "Julian—Martha, Edith, and I have given you a brief rundown on today's socioeconomic system. Government, if you can call it that, is largely in the hands of the Production Congress composed of representatives from all the guilds, which represent every necessary type of endeavor. Aside from local civic government, there is a skeleton national government, which you might compare to the House of Lords and the Queen and Royal Family of England at the time you went into stasis. Mostly show. A leftover from the past society, just as the Queen and the House of Lords were leftovers from feudalism.''

''All right, you've already told me about that.''

''Very well. I am prominent in a group that wishes to take a further step in attaining a society that will fulfill the promises and hopes that are at the root of our whole human civilization.''

''And that step is. . . ?''

''World government. You see, there are three of what you used to call 'world powers' existing today. There are some minor differences in our socio-economic systems, but they are only minor. My associates and I believe it is time to take the step of uniting these three: United America, Common Europe, and the Soviet Complex. Once that is accomplished, one by one the so-called undeveloped countries will certainly apply for admission. Some of the small states that still exist in the East, the Near East, South America, and especially Africa, can only follow.''

''Why is all this important?''

''Amalgamating the three great powers would join our technologies and bring greater efficiency. There would be one great Production Congress, rather than three. And, so far as I see, the anachronistic national civic governments could be allowed to wither away completely, since there would no longer be foreign countries to deal with, with their ambassadors, consuls and so forth."

Julian said, "That brings something else to mind. What's happened to the underdeveloped countries in the last thirty years?"

"They are still largely undeveloped and backward. There are still small nations in, say, the Near East that are absolute monarchies—sheikdoms. As the value of oil decreases in the world, they become ever poorer. There are still military dictatorships in South America; their economies, unable to compete on such world markets as remain, subject their peoples to worse and worse poverty."

"Then why would you want to take them into this new world government you advocate? They'd drag down the level of the advanced countries if you automatically put them on your same Guaranteed Annual Income."

The other looked at him levelly. "Because they are members of the human race. To the question, 'Am I my brother's keeper?', Julian, the answer is yes. Nor is it a question of their coming to us as beggars, at least most of them. These undeveloped countries have been unable to industrialize, not being able to compete with the economies of the advanced countries, but they are sources of raw materials. And many offer a great deal in very desirable localities for residential areas, in scenic areas for travelers, in areas to be converted into great World Parks. I, for instance, would love to see the whole Congo turned back to nature, reseeded with animal life ranging from gorillas to elephants."

Julian nodded. "Tell me, Raymond, in this present society, what happens to the crackpot genius? Take Edison. I understand he had less than a year of schooling. Certainly the Aptitude Quotient computers wouldn't have selected him."

Leete chuckled. "I am afraid genius, crackpot or otherwise, will out in any society. For one thing, your Edison would have gotten more than a few months' education today. But even if the computers had not selected him, his urge toward experimentation would have come out in his studies in his leisure time. As I said, genius will out. Both Leonardo da Vinci and Michelangelo were born underprivileged, and in one of the most restrictive societies man has ever had—feudalism. It didn't prevent them from turning out some of the greatest work man has ever accomplished."

Julian took a breath. "All right. Another question. Why are you people so down on religion?"

The other looked at him in amazement. "We're not down on religion. You can practice any religion you wish."

"Then why do so few seem to?"

"Julian, it had already begun in your day. How many of your intelligent and educated friends really believed in the old fundamentalist or orthodox religions? I don't mean just lip service, but believing the whole story?"

"I was raised an Episcopalian. I didn't pay a great deal of attention to it, perhaps, but basically I believed in the Christian religion."

"Oh, you did, eh? You know, Julian, for a long time I've held the belief that any philosophy, religion, or political belief can be summed up in two hundred words. If it can't, something is wrong with it. Very well. Sit down at the desk there and give me the Judeo-Christian religion in two hundred words."

Julian scowled at him, but obeyed. He sat down at his desk, and instead of utilizing the voco-typer, took up a stylo and paper. He began to write. He soon found two hundred words weren't a great deal. He scratched out some of the sentences but persevered. He must have sat for the better part of an hour before finishing. But when he reread what he had written, and reread it again, he took up the three or four sheets of paper, crumpled them and threw them into the wastepaper basket.

He returned to the chair opposite the doctor.

He said sourly, "Anybody who had never heard of the Christian religion and read that would think I was an idiot if I believed it."

Leete said, his voice wry, "You know, most of our Earth religions have subscribed to the idea that God, or the gods, created man in his own image and is highly concerned with him. But now we are tending to the belief that man is far from alone in being an intelligent creature in the universe; that most likely there are other intelligent life forms far in advance of ours. Somebody somewhere pointed out that if there are gods whose chief concern is man, they can't be very important gods, considering the extent of the universe."

Julian grunted amusement. He said, "I've heard of

the attempts to contact extraterrestrial intelligent life.''

''Yes, it is just a matter of time, I suppose. There's one interesting aspect of religion that I've considered that I suspect few religious persons have. Specifically, suppose that there is a God, and that he isn't benevolent.''

''How do you mean?''

''Obviously, such a being would be far, far further above us than, say, we are above the cockroach. And we would be less capable of understanding him than the cockroach is of understanding us. We would have no idea what motivates him.''

Julian regarded him blankly.

Leete chuckled. ''Take, for instance, the cow as it was before you went into stasis. Cows, had they been capable of thought, might have thought of we humans as gods since we fed them, housed them, protected them from enemies, took care of their health, even helped bring their offspring into the world. Surely they would have thought of us as benevolent. In actuality, we stole their milk all their lives, and finally wound up killing and eating them.''

Julian said, ''We seem to have drifted far from our original subject of why our apartments are being bugged, world government, and socioeconomic systems. I'm still not sure just what label this system would bear.''

The other said humorously, ''When I was a young fellow there was a science fiction editor named John C. Campbell who once wrote that any socioeconomic system will work well given top men to run it. Both heaven and hell are despotisms. Today, with our computers and data banks, we have the means to find the best men to direct the workings of our society. However, I far from agree with Campbell. For instance, it is my belief that if instead of Nixon and his people at the helm of American government at the time you went into hibernation, you'd had Jesus for president and his twelve disciples for a cabinet, the country would still have gone to pot. The politico-economic system no longer worked, and nobody could have made it work. For one——"

But at that point the identity screen buzzed. When they looked up, they saw it was Edith.

Chapter Sixteen

The Year 2, New Calendar

And this, too, shall pass away. . . . How much this expresses! How chastening in the hour of pride! How consoling in the depths of affliction! . . . And yet, let us hope, rather, it is not quite true. Let us hope that by the best cultivation of the physical world beneath and around us, and the best intellectual and moral world within us, we shall secure an individual, social, and political prosperity and happiness, whose course shall be onward and upward, and which, while the earth endures, shall not pass away.

—Abraham Lincoln

EDITH ENTERED and looked at them in mock-suspicion. "What are you two up to now?"

Julian got to his feet and said severely, "Young lady, why aren't you at work? Somebody has to toil while we who are on Guaranteed Annual Income loll about frittering away our time."

She made a small curtsey. "I've finished my stint,

you malingerers. And what's more, I'm tired of sitting before those console screens. How about a walk, Jule?"

"Nothing would suit me more. Besides, there's something I wanted to talk to you about." Julian turned to her father. "When you tell Mrs. Leete, be sure it's either in the bath, with the shower turned on, or somewhere out in the open."

"Very well, Julian."

He said, "There's something else I wanted to ask you about. . . . Oh, yes. Why didn't you inform Security about the two attacks?"

"Because I suspected the attempts were made so that I would complain, so that it would get into the news and focus attention on the rival group which, thus far, has had precious little attention paid to it. They want as much publicity as they can get. Why should I help them?"

"That kind of publicity?"

"They want to play themselves up as rough and tough, a return to the old type of society where men were ruthless and fought their way to the top, rather than being selected by cold machines."

Julian nodded and turned to Edith. "Shall we go?"

She looked from one to the other. "What's been going on?"

"I'll tell you as we walk," he said. "See you later Raymond."

Going down in the elevator, Edith, frowning slightly, asked, "What were you discussing with Father?"

He didn't really expect the elevator compartment

to be bugged, but he shook his head. "Tell you later, Edie."

"It gets mysteriouser and mysteriouser."

Once out of the building, they crossed over to the park beyond and ambled along one of the gravel paths. Each of the university city's high-rise apartment buildings were surrounded by approximately a square mile of parks, pools, woods, and small streams, somewhat reminiscent in Julian's eye of a combination swank golf course and the gardens of the country estate of a British duke. There were quite a few other pedestrians taking advantage of the superlative day, but the area was large enough that it was in no sense crowded.

"Where are we going?" he asked.

She grinned mischievously. "Somewhere you'll never believe. To the Mythological and Prehistoric Zoo."

"Sounds something like Disneyland." When he saw that struck no chord, he said, "It was the largest of the amusement parks in my day. For kids, actually. At least, so they said."

"This is for young people too, but also for older scholars."

"When do we get to it?"

"We're already there. Look," she pointed.

His eyes popped. At first, he thought the small heard grazing in an attractive glen to be horses, but then he realized that each had a single horn projecting from its forehead and that they seemed more delicate, more gentle than the average horse.

He laughed at himself, at his surprise, and said,

"What a clever job. Attaching those horns so that they look like unicorns."

She smiled at him. "They are unicorns. Those are real horns."

"Come off it! The unicorn was a mythical beast."

"I told you this is the Mythological and Prehistoric Zoo."

He looked at her, then the unicorns, then back at her.

She laughed at him in such a way that it was obvious that she had expected to laugh at him at this stage. She said, "Come over this way. We'll see the mammoths."

"Mammoths! They've been extinct for . . . for a million years!"

"No. Not really. We have cave paintings depicting Cro-Magnon Man hunting them. Mastadons, too. We're particularly proud of the job we've been able to do on the mammoths. Four were found, frozen in the ice, in Siberia, in almost perfect condition. So perfect that the meat was actually edible. At any rate, the specialists in that branch of biology didn't have to guess and were able to reconstruct them just about perfectly."

He stopped in his tracks. "What in the name of everything are you talking about?"

"Jule, Jule, come along. Man has been changing animals around since prehistoric times. Look at the dog. Heaven only knows what he originally looked like. But centuries before we had ever heard of genetical engineering, we had bred the dog from the size of a Pekingese to a Great Dane and back again. They're the same species, of course. You can cross a Peke and a Great Dane.''

''What's that got to do with a mammoth? This I've got to see!''

''Let's go, then. They're over here. In actuality, there isn't much to see. They look like elephants with hair and overgrown tusks.''

''You just let them run around?''

She laughed. ''They're not carnivorous, you know. Now, the saber-toothed tiger is another thing. So is our tyrannosaurus. You'll be amazed at the size of the pit and cage we've had to put him in. The brontosaurus is something else again. Herbivorous, of course, so we have him in a duplication of the environment he must have lived in, sort of a swamp. They had to guess a lot about the dinosaurs; all we have are skeletons to work with. The same with the dragons. The biologists made them herbivorous too, just to make them easier to handle.''

''Dragons! I suppose they breathe fire?'' Julian added sarcastically after his initial reaction. ''Who are you trying to kid, Edie?''

She had to laugh at that. ''Well, no, they don't breathe fire, much to the disappointment of some of the children. The Pegasus also has the scientists stumped. You simply can't get enough wingspread on an animal as big as a horse to enable it to fly. There—over there are your mammoths.''

Julian gaped. There were six of them, and Edith had been right. They were about the size of Indian Elephants, had long tusks possibly ten feet in length which curved in a unique spiral, and were covered

with yellowish brown woolly hair which reached almost to the ground. They seemed docile enough.

Julian shook his head and turned his stare to her.
"All right, at least brief me. Are these things living,
or are they just clever robots, like they had in that
Disneyland I mentioned?"

"No, they're living. We've come a long way since
that immunochemist Oswald Avery came up with
deoxyribose nucleic acid, or DNA, and the scientists
of your period created life in the laboratory."

"Nobody had created life in the laboratory in my
day. Not to speak of dragons."

"Oh," she said, frowning. "My memory was that
in 1965 a team at the University of Illinois, under a
Professor Sol Spiegelman, succeeded in putting together the non-living nucleic-acid message which
produced a virus which would go on and multiply
indefinitely. Their artificial virus was completely in-
distinguishable from a natural virus. Of course, it's a
matter of whether or not you consider a virus alive.
At any rate, progress was geometric in the field from
then on."

He said weakly, "Let's sit down on this bench for
awhile. I could use a little breather before being
taken to see a Tyrannosaurus. Are you telling me that
your modern biologists can create, in the laboratory,
just about any type of life form you want?"

"Why, yes. For over ten years now."

"Even a man?"

"Yes. Though that's in the way of being a taboo.
We tread very carefully in this field, Jule. The scientists are possibly a bit more humble today than they
were a third of a century ago. But cloning has become
a reality. You see, every cell in the body of any

organism carries all the information needed to construct whole organs, or indeed, the body itself. I believe Father told you that we no longer transplant organs. The geneticists simply take a few cells from any part of a sick man and grow duplicates of his defective organs from them. They call it autoplantation. That, of course, is a somewhat different field than the making of new life forms.''

"I'm completely confused. I read a little about this sort of thing in articles in *Time* and *Newsweek* and such before I went into hibernation. In fact, I recall an article by some science popularizer—Isaac Asimov, I think his name was—in which he mentioned the possibility of upping the chimp, or some other of the higher apes, to where it could think and even talk to the point where we could make slaves of them. Have them do the drudgery jobs, such as assembly-line work. And he mentioned the possibility of putting a voice box in the dog, so that our pets could talk. Things like that. Has that happened?''

She said, scowling slightly, ''It's all possible, but not usual. For one thing, our cousin the chimpanzee isn't practical. That is, not as efficient as a robot. He doesn't have an opposed thumb. And he is short-lived and clumsy. Talking dogs or, say, horses? Who wants to talk to a horse? Dogs? In actuality, I have seen a few talking dogs, but I've never been comfortable with them, even those who have also had their intelligence increased. I love dogs the way they have always been, man's comrade. It always sets me back to have them tell me good morning. However, there are other things that make more sense.''

''Such as?''

''Growing arms and hands on dolphins, so that

they can perform underwater tasks."

He closed his eyes in pain. "Why not just switch man around so that he has gills and can breathe underwater?"

"That too is quite possible. However, man is a land animal, Jule. I told you how much we fear playing God."

He said, "My mind is reeling. Look, in this mythological zoo things do you have, say mermaids and centaurs?"

"No, nor the sphinx—a man's head on a lion's body—though it would be possible to create them. However, we have no desire to make such mockeries of men. Theoretically, I suppose, they could come up with a vampire of the Dracula school." She thought about it, her mouth twisted in amusement. "The basic requirements would be a man-type creature that was allergic to daylight and who could live on blood."

"Live on blood! Come on now. No mammal could live on a blood diet."

"Vampire bats do, don't they? Those down in the tropics of Mexico. Also that tribe of Africans, the Masai, or whatever their name was . . . didn't they live on an exclusive diet of cow's blood and milk? That's fairly near to it. Perhaps they'd have to feed our artificially manufactured vampire vitamin and mineral supplements or something."

Julian attempted to enter into the spirit of the thing. "But sun allergy and living on blood were only two of the requirements. How about killing them by driving a stake through their hearts, or shooting them with a silver bullet?"

"I'd think either method would be effective with just about any human-type creature, vampire or otherwise."

"Well, how about them being able to turn themselves into either a bat or a wolf?"

It was her turn to laugh. "I surrender. I think science will have to experiment around a bit more before that would be possible."

"I'd hate to see them turn out even the abbreviated vampire you say is now possible."

"Good heavens, sir, I didn't say they would; I simply said they *could*."

"I don't know how we got off this track. But this genetic engineering, as you called it. . . . If your biologists and genetic engineers can mess around with life to this extent, why don't you, say, double the I.Q.—or triple it, for that matter—of every new child born?"

"It's been considered. In fact, the debate still goes on, and possibly will for years. I told you they were treading carefully, Jule. You see, we're a bit leery of having the godhead turned over to the race."

"Well, certainly, if it were possible to assure that every new child born had an I.Q. of at least one-hundred fifty. . . ."

Edith sighed before interrupting him. "That's the basic problem, Jule. What would you rather be, smart or happy?"

He regarded her dubiously. "Are they necessarily in conflict with each other?"

"That's what we don't know. Let us say that one hundred is the average intelligent quotient. A person with an I.Q. of fifty is most likely an unhappy person.

But is a person with an I.Q. of one-hundred fifty also out of step with society? Not to speak of one with an I.Q. of two-hundred or even higher.''

"Damned if I know, but if everyone was upped to an I.Q. of two-hundred, they'd all be in the same boat.''

She nodded. "That's the way the argument goes. But there are ramifications. For instance, when I was a young girl, for some reason not clear to me now, everybody wanted to be tall. Especially men wanted to be at least six feet. A man six-feet-four, or taller, was particularly admired. Why? Why was the Swede with an average height of something like six feet considered superior to, say, a Japanese, whose average was a bit over five feet? At the time of their conquest, the Aztecs averaged less than five feet, their women about four feet, eight inches. It didn't seem to be a handicap.''

He shook his head. "I never thought about it.''

She said, "The world is still overpopulated. Why don't we let our genetic engineers breed down the size of our people to three feet? It would save both food and room. Our houses, our cars, everything could become one half the size, use one half the materials to construct.''

"Why three feet?'' he complained. "Why not one foot?''

"Why not? That's the question. When man issued forth from the caves a few thousand years ago, it was necessary for him to be as big as possible to fight off his animal enemies, and as smart as possible to solve the problems that confronted him. It seems unlikely that the very earliest man was much smarter than, say, the chimpanzee and probably not too much larger. He upgraded himself through natural selection. Those who were smaller were killed off, both by animals and by his fellow man. He was also eliminated from breeding, because the larger males took all the desirable, healthy females. The same applied to I.Q. The more stupid fell by the wayside, leaving the more intelligent to breed and pass on their genes."

"That's pretty basic—and obvious."

"Very well, Jule. The question now becomes, in this age, why should being either big, or more intelligent, be desirable?"

"This is the damnedest debate I think I've ever been in. Ever since I was a child, I wanted to be a good physical specimen and as smart as possible."

"I didn't say anything against being a good physical specimen. Size has nothing to do with that. But there's your basic question. Would man be happier if he had an average I.Q. of two-hundred, or three-thousand, or whatever? And that is one of the big questions being argued by our best authorities on the matter."

"And what answers do they come up with?"

"None, so far. We are in no hurry. As I told you, we have become more humble of recent decades. We are very cold-bloodedly deciding where we want to go, and trying to decide whether future generations will agree with the path we choose. We are *very* humble, Jule."

He said, "Every day that passes, I come up against things that flabbergast me. What do you say we go on? Not only do I want to see a saber-toothed tiger, but I'm just dying to examine what your biologists have cooked up in the way of a dragon." He added, grinning, "By the way, they haven't come up with a Push-You-Pull-Me, have they? A mythical beast out of Doctor Doolittle?"

"I'm sorry. That one escapes me."

"You've neglected some required childhood reading. It was an animal that looked somewhat like a horse, and had a head on each end."

It was her turn to look blank. "How did it——"

"Damned if I know. I never figured it out."

She smiled. "Well, let's go see the sabertooth."

He said, "Just a moment. First, possibly we should talk about that discussion I was having with your Father."

She settled back into her seat on the bench. "I forgot. It's always so fascinating to bring these new things to you."

He said very deliberately, "Your apartment and mine have been bugged. That is, someone has tapped both our TV phones, and has installed electronic devices that enable them to hear every conversation that takes place in your apartment. I've gimmicked the one bug they had in my place, but I assume they'll either try to repair it or put a new one in shortly."

She eyed him. "But . . . who?"

"I'm not sure, but I have my suspicions. Your father is evidently knee-deep in what we would have called 'politics' in my time."

Her eyes turned thoughtful.

Julian said softly, "I lied to young Sean the other day."

Her forehead wrinkled. "How do you mean?"

"I know of at least ten persons I have killed. At least. Men, women, and . . . one child. In the last case, we were racing through a small hamlet, scared to death, anything that moved . . ."

"What are you talking about? You sound half out of your mind."

"I'm talking about the fact that for some reason which I don't understand, because I'm out of my depth in this world of yours, somebody is making an attempt on your father's life. And, so far as I know, I am probably the most competent bodyguard alive in United America."

"You're insane!"

"Yes, you said that. Now, this is what I need. You say you are a student of anthropology and archaeology. I assume you have access to museums. I want a high-calibered handgun, a nine-millimeter Luger or a .45 Colt. I want at least twenty rounds of ammunition for it and two clips, magazines, the things that hold the cartridges. I also need a combat knife . . . a trench knife, they sometimes call them. I don't know what you'll be able to steal out of the museums in this immediate vicinity. If you can get more than one trench knife, try to do so, so I can have a choice. The German ones can be used as throwing knives, as well as a close-combat weapon. That's the one I would prefer, but do the best you can."

"You're mad!"

"Yes, of course. And your father's life, and mine, and possibly yours are in immediate danger. I haven't the vaguest idea in hell why."

"But if someone hated my father so much, why haven't they already killed him?"

"Possibly they've already tried and were too inept. In the past few days he's been mugged and an attempt made to wreck his car while he was going at high speed. Get the gun and trench knife, Edith. Immediately. And now let's go see that sabertooth, and the dragons. I still can't believe it."

Chapter Seventeen

The Year 1940

THERE SEEMED TO BE somewhat of a change in the quality of Julian West's dreams since he had arrived in the twenty-first century, rather, the First Century, New Calendar, as they called it now. From time to time he had flashbacks to yesteryear that weren't particularly nightmares, but simply a reliving of the past. But no, this particular one was a nightmare.

It had been on a trip from their Miami Beach home to Nassau, in the Bahamas, on his father's yacht, *Go West*, a one-hundred twenty-foot motor cruiser. Barry and Betty West had invited three other couples, and Julian, who was only six or seven at the time, was allowed to come. The crew consisted of six: the captain, the engineer, two hands and two in the steward department. The captain and engineer were full-time employees, but Barry West made it a practice to hire the hands only when he planned a cruise. The two stewards, one of whom doubled as cook, were employees in the West mansion in Miami Beach and were drafted each time the *Go West* shipped out. It wasn't a matter of expense; the Wests simply liked to be in the care of servants who knew exactly how they liked things.

The dream began early in the morning.

Julian, who had a small stateroom of his own toward the stern, had awakened and dressed himself, and momentarily considered going to the master stateroom up foreward to see if his mother and father would invite him into their bed for a romp. But no, he decided, they had all been drinking very heavily the day before, and he had been able to hear them late into the night. It was nothing new; he would be hard put to remember an evening when his parents weren't wobbly with drink. He then considered going to the galley and seeing if Edward was available to talk to. But no, Edward would probably be busy getting ready for breakfast. If past cruises were any criteria, breakfast would stretch over several hours as the hungover guests emerged one by one from their cabins.

Edward was a favorite of little Julian's—one of the few West servants who, when they were alone, treated him as an individual rather than as "the young master." He spent as much time as Edward could find free talking to the middle-aged, sad-faced servant. Edward had been around for as long as Julian could remember, which was exceptional in the West household. Servants were apt to come and go, particularly when one or the other or both of the Wild Wests got on a nasty binge.

Julian decided instead to go up to the bridge and see if the captain would let him play around the ship's controls. Perhaps he could even steer. He loved to steer and usually Captain Fielding didn't mind on a clear day when the sea wasn't too choppy.

He made his way up to the deck and then climbed the aft ladderway to the sundeck. For a time he stood at the fantail rail. The overcast was starting to burn off and the sea was beginning to glint. The yacht was quartering into a northeast wind, the propellers churning up the impossibly blue Bahama waters. Three gulls followed gracefully. He knew that had it been night, there would be a faint green-white phosphorescence in the wake.

He turned and went forward to the topside controls, forward of the sundeck. But the captain wasn't there. The yacht was on autopilot and one of the seamen, the one called Jack, was on watch. Julian instinctively knew that Jack didn't like small boys, even if he was in no position to do or say anything about it.

Julian took the co-pilot seat and sat there awhile, his hands in his lap. They were already in the Bahama archipelago, and passing through scores of small islands and islets, coral reefs and shoals. From time to time he could spot colorful birds and once they passed fifteen pelicans standing on a bar in a straight line in a couple of inches of water.

Julian stood on the co-pilot seat and lifted the two sight vanes of the pelorus atop the gyrocompass. He moved the pelorus around so that he could take a bearing on a small lighthouse on an islet about a mile off. Captain Fielding had shown him how to take a bearing. He wasn't quite sure *why* you took a bearing, but he knew it was part of running the ship and he was proud that he could do it.

Jack said grumpily, "Maybe you shouldn't do that, boy."

Julian looked at the other levelly for a moment. The man had seen Julian playing with the pelorus before, when the captain was present. However, Julian was in no mood to make an issue of it. Even at this early time in life he disliked controversy and avoided it when he could. It was probably a reaction against all the tiffs, the emotional crises, the verbal brawls that were almost the daily diet of the West family.

He got down from the seat without a word and left. He went down to the lounge and found that there was still no one up. He passed through it, and walked past the galley. He peered in but both his friend Edward and the cook were much too busy to bother with him. He went on down the corridor to the master bedroom. He'd peer in and see if Barry and Betty were still asleep.

The door was not locked. He opened it and peeked inside. The curtains were drawn at the portholes and the room very dim, but he could make out his father's form in the bed, though not his mother's. He could hear water running in the bathroom. Hesitantly, he crept in to check if Barry West was still asleep.

He approached the side of the bed quietly.

And then the door to the bath opened and a woman came out, a woman who was completely naked. At first he thought it was his mother but then he realized with a shock that this woman was a brunette; his mother was blonde.

He shrank back. A closet door, half open, was immediately behind him. She hadn't seen him as yet. He backed into the closet and softly closed the door until it was only open a crack. Where was his mother?

Humming softly, the woman approached the bed. The air conditioning wasn't on, since nights were cool on the ocean, but the sun had come up by now and Barry West, who habitually slept nude, had pushed aside the bedsheet.

Julian could recognize her now. It was Mrs. Simmons. She was younger than the other guests, and Julian had thought her very pretty. She had done a good deal of gushing over him when he had been presented to her; but he had liked her anyway. Most grown-ups gushed; you got used to it.

His eyes rounded and he held a hand over his mouth when she reached down to touch his father.

Although Julian couldn't see his eyes open in the dimness, his father evidently awoke. He jerked into a half-sitting position and yelped, "Why, you little devil you! Didn't you have enough last night?"

Mrs. Simmons giggled and said something in a low, husky voice that Julian couldn't hear.

Where was his mother? Could she possibly be in some other cabin—doing things like this with one of the other guests?

He was about to dash out of the closet and away from the room. But just then a perfunctory knock came at the door and before Mrs. Simmons could jerk away, the door opened and Edward came in, carrying bedding.

He stood there a moment in confusion, then stammered, "I'm sorry, sir. I thought you were topside, sir. I . . . I . . ."

Mrs. Simmons had turned her head away and put her hands over her face.

But Barry West, in a high rage, scrambled from the bed and stood up. He roared, "Get out of here, you goddamned ass! Get out! Get out!"

Edward whirled and stumbled out, hurriedly closing the door behind him.

Julian closed the closet door completely and backed as far into the closet as he could, trembling all over.

In the stateroom beyond, he could hear voices, his father's shaking in anger, but with a tone of soothing reassurance. And he could hear clothing rustling. He hoped beyond all hope that there would be no need for Barry West to get something from this closet.

His prayer was answered, since after about ten minutes there were no more sounds from the cabin. Julian carefully edged the door open just a trifle. There was no one in the stateroom. He crept out and hurried for the door.

As he ran down the corridor, breathing heavily, his mother came out of one of the guest cabins. She was dressed in a night robe, and, as always, looked so pretty to the young boy.

She eyed Julian with surprise. "Why, Jule, what are you doing up and around?"

He stuttered a bit and managed to say, "I . . . I was just going up to the bridge, Mama. Uh, to see if the captain would let me steer."

She looked at him. "Well, run along. I'll be up for breakfast a little later."

When he got back up to the sundeck, he was still terribly shaken. They were entering the beautiful Nassau harbor, heading for the Prince George Wharf. He had been to Nassau once before and knew the routine. The captain would be on the bridge now, directing the docking, asking for port instructions on the FM-UHF marine radio, handling the wheel himself. He would have no time for little Julian, who would only be in the way. Julian remained where he was, watching.

A docking always fascinated him. Jack was up forward and the other crewman in the stern, both with coils of rope in their hands. As they came in slowly, neatly, to within a few yards of the dock, the crewmen heaved their lines and the shore hands on the dock grabbed them up and dropped the loops over the iron bollards. The deck winches grumbled and took in the slack of the lines and slowly snubbed the length of the yacht against the wharf. More lines went out. The deep groaning of the engines stopped. The two crewmen hurried midship and shortly the gangplank was swung out and latched.

His father joined him. He was scowling, obviously still irritated. And Jules knew the reason. He was dressed in yachting clothing, including an officer's cap.

He asked, "Have you had breakfast, Jule?"

"No, Daddy."

"Don't call me Daddy, for Christ's sake, it makes me feel old. Call me Father. Come along, we'll get something to eat and then go ashore. I have some things to do before it gets too goddamned hot."

They went into the small dining room, across from the galley, and the cook himself served them.

"Where in the hell's that stupid bastard Edward?" Barry West demanded.

"I don't know, sir," the cook told him.

Julian suspected that Edward was keeping as far away from his father as possible, hoping the ship's owner would cool off.

Barry West at the age of thirty was a handsome man, although there was a somewhat petulant quality about his mouth. However, when he had a hangover, or was more than ordinarily upset about something, young Julian hated to look at him. He was capable of bad tempers and on the few occasions he had physically punished his son, it had been more violent than the size of the boy warranted.

They ate their breakfast in silence, except for Barry West's comment, "I don't know why in the hell I'm letting you tag along. I suppose it won't do you any harm to stretch your legs a bit."

Julian didn't say anything to that. He would just as well not have accompanied his parent, but he was afraid to say so for fear of irritating the other still further.

Ashore, they headed down the wharf and in the direction of Bay Street. The last time they had been in Nassau, it was his mother who had taken Julian ashore. She had had some shopping to do and his father had been too drunk to accompany them. In fact, he hadn't gone ashore for the full time they had been on the island of New Providence.

The souvenir and other stores fascinated Julian. They had touristy names, and merchandise to go with them. The Trade Winds, the Island Shop, the English China House, Solomon's Mines, the Nassau Shop, the John Bull. The bars had names such as Blackbeard's Tavern and Dirty Dick's. The souvenirs consisted of lots of straw things, hats, dolls, postcards, pillows with *Nassau* painted in large letters upon them, canes with *Nassau* burnt into their length, but above all, things of straw.

His father had him by the hand, hurrying him along through the pedestrians, impatient with the boy's attempt to look at the store displays.

Then he stopped abruptly. "What in the hell are you doing off the yacht?"

It was Edward, a look of consternation on his face. He was carrying two packages.

He said, "The captain gave me permission, Mr. West. I had promised my wife I'd pick up a souvenir for her and one for my little girl."

"Oh, he did, eh? Well, listen here, Mr. Peeping Tom, you can just go back to the ship and pack your things and get the hell off. Get what pay's coming to you from Captain Fielding, but be the hell off the yacht by the time I get back."

The other, a tremble in his voice, pleaded, "Sir, please. I need the job. I've been with you for a long time. Jobs aren't the easiest thing in the world to get these days. Especially at my age."

"My heart is bleeding for you," Barry West snarled. "Get your pay and get off the ship."

"Mr. West, the amount of pay I have coming isn't even enough to get me back to Miami and my family."

"That's no damned skin off my nose," Julian's father said. "Come on, Jule." He pulled the boy by the hand.

Julian looked back over his shoulder in despair.

His friend said, "Good-bye, Julian."

"Good-bye, Edward," Julian responded miserably.

"Shut up and keep moving," said his father.

It was then the dream ended. With the realization that he did not like his father and mother, Julian woke up.

Chapter Eighteen

The Year 2, New Calendar

I pray that the imagination we uncloak for defense and arms and outer space may yet be uncloaked as well for grace and beauty in our daily lives. As an economy, we need it. As a society, we shall perish without it.
                              —Adlai Stevenson

Revolutions are not made; they come. A revolution is as natural a growth as an oak. It comes out of the past. Its foundations are laid far back.
                              —Wendell Phillips

HE WAS NOT IN the usual sweat brought on by the nightmares filled with memories of blood and horror and human suffering, but he was quite distressed.

Edith, her head on the pillow next to him, asked, "What's wrong, Jule?"

"Bit of a nightmare, I guess," he told her. "Nothing."

"Nothing? You mean to tell me you have upsetting dreams?"

"'Upsetting dreams' is a gentle way of putting it. I've had them all my life, these nightmares. They're evidently more vivid than most people's from what all the headshrinkers have told me."

She sat up in bed. She hadn't bothered to put on a nightgown before they fell asleep. Her body was superb, but right now he was in no mood for sex.

She said, "We must go and see Father immediately!"

"Why?"

But she had already hurried from the bed in the direction of the apartment's order box to send for clothing. She said over her shoulder, "To tell him about your dreams."

He shrugged, but got himself up and went into the bath. He in no way wanted to discuss his nightmares with Dr. Leete, but he supposed there was no choice. Supposedly he was still under medical care.

Dressed, they didn't take their breakfast in his apartment but headed immediately down the hall to the Leete quarters. He hadn't the vaguest idea what Edith's father and mother thought about his relationship with their daughter. In his own time, people had at least paid lip service to appearances. But here he was, sleeping with Edith, and seemingly it was of no importance whatsoever to them. Well, at least hypocrisy wasn't involved; certainly that was progress in the development of human relations.

The academician, his expression disgruntled, was

staring into the library booster screen on the living room desk. He looked up when Edith and Julian entered.

"Ridiculous!" he said, gesturing at the screen.

"What's ridiculous, Father?" Edith asked.

He looked at her, closing one eye in disgust. "My looking at the news. Every time I do, I become irritated."

She sighed as though she had been through this before. "What is the world currently doing that you disapprove of?"

"This star probe to the Alpha Centauri system. Ridiculous!"

Julian asked with some surprise, "Has the space program gotten to that point?"

"No. That's why it's ridiculous," Leete said. "Do you know what that robot spacecraft will find when it gets to Alpha Centauri A and Alpha Centauri B, assuming that the two companion stars have habitable planets?"

"No. What?"

"It'll find men who have been there possibly for years."

"Whatever are you talking about, Father?"

"About going off half-cocked. Why not wait another decade or two until we know more about space drive? What's the hurry? It's the same story all over again. Back in the 1950s when the United States and the Soviet Union began exploring space, instead of getting together—and utilizing German and British science as well—America went racing off. Billions upon billions of dollars, billions of man-hours of our top scientists and technicians, millions of tons of materials that were needed elsewhere."

Julian said, "They made it, though. Landing a man on the moon was one of the biggest events in my time."

The academician flicked off the screen in a gesture of disgust. "They made it; they put a man on the moon—two men, as I recall. Now, suppose they had taken their time, amalgamated their efforts with the Russians and any other interested countries: united effort would have cut the cost in half, and twice as much probably would have been learned."

Edith said patiently, "What has that got to do with the Alpha Centauri probe?"

"It's the same situation. What's the hurry? In ten years we will have twice the information we have now. For all I know, we'll have figured out a faster-than-light drive. By the time this ridiculous robot space probe gets to the vicinity, there'll already be men there, waiting for it—if there's any suitable place there for waiting."

Julian was out of his depth, as usual.

"All right," Edith said. "According to Stephen Dole, the F2 to K1 stars are of the spectral classes that might be suitable for the nurturing of planets habitable by mankind, planets that can be colonized. Sooner or later, we've got to reach out. This is the first step."

"But premature! What is the damned hurry? Only twenty-five thousand years ago, we were painting bison and deer on the walls and ceilings of our caves. Why can't we slow down a bit these days and wait until we've progressed a little further before sending out inadequate expeditions that will be anachronisms five years after they've taken off?''

Edith said, ''Perhaps you're right. However, we've got another problem on our hands at this moment. Jule has recurring nightmares.''

''Nightmares? In this day and age?''

Julian said wearily, ''Remember, I'm not of this day and age.''

''Why didn't you tell me sooner?''

Edith interrupted, ''I've got an errand to run for Jule. When this project began, our job was to take care of him as if he were a four-year-old child. Now we've gotten to the point where we're running around on *his* projects.'' She grinned at him to take the edge off her words, then turned to leave. ''I'll pick up breakfast somewhere along the way. I want to get to the museum when it first opens.''

When she was gone, the doctor waited for Julian to begin.

''It's nothing important. I've had them since I was a kid. Very vivid. I usually wake up sweating. I saw an auto accident once when I was about twelve years old. Four people killed. They looked like mincemeat. The first dead persons I had ever seen. I've dreamed about it since then about once every two months. I know it's abnormal, but I've been to a multitude of doctors, from psychiatrists to acupuncture specialists, and it's never done me any good.''

''But that was over thirty years ago, Julian. Today, we can not only cure you of your nightmares but give you a new set of pleasant dreams to order.''

''Give me dreams?''

''Yes, of course. Programmed dreams. Anything from pleasant dreams of childhood, to dreams of heroic deeds with you the hero. How would you like to be Horatius at the Bridge? Or we can give you erotic fantasies beyond your wildest dreams." The academician chuckled at his own joke. "Now, I'm not suggesting that you turn to sleep to get your sexual release, but it can and has been done."

Julian slumped in his chair. "This has been the cross I've borne all my life. How often have you killed an eight-year-old child, Raymond? I do it vividly about once a month."

"I'll get right on it."

The doctor put a call through to Vienna with Julian watching, hardly daring to breathe. To be cured of the exhausting, terrifying dreams that he'd had as far back as he could remember!

Leete turned to him and indicated the phone screen. He had been speaking into it in Interlingua and using medical terminology with which Julian was unfamiliar.

"Doctor Oswaldo Schon wishes to speak with you."

The face in the screen was typically Germanic, thin with very intense blue eyes.

"It is very interesting to speak to you, Mr. West," Dr. Schon said in excellent English. "Some time in the future, when you are more adjusted to your new environment, I would enjoy an opportunity to discuss medical practice of a third of a century ago."

"It would be a pleasure, Doctor," Julian replied.

The other asked him a series of questions which didn't seem to probe too deeply. Evidently it wasn't even necessary to see the patient in person. Finally, he asked to speak to Academician Leete again. The conversation swung back to Interlingua, and Dr. Leete took several notes before switching off the phone.

He turned to Julian. "Evidently a very routine matter. I'll see about the prescription immediately and treat you before evening."

Julian expressed his great relief, then said, "I'm surprised at how many people speak English—even this Austrian."

Leete chuckled. "He wasn't speaking English; he was speaking Interlingua. The computer translated his Interlingua into English for you, and your English into Interlingua for him. You could talk to an Eskimo if you wished, and his tribal tongue would be translated into English for you."

Julian shook his head. "They were just beginning to experiment with computer translaters when I went under." He shifted in his chair and said by way of changing the subject, "There have been a few questions that have accumulated that I wanted to ask you about."

"Of course."

"Edith mentioned the other day that if someone wanted to read pornography, he could do so until his eyes dropped out. Would that apply to everybody? Even to a six-year-old child?"

"Why yes, certainly. A six-year-old usually can't read any too well, even with our modern means of education, but if he was interested in books on sex, pornography or otherwise, I suppose he could look at the pictures."

Julian was unhappy with that answer. "As a doctor, don't you think that would be bad for the child?"

"Why? There's nothing wrong with sex, and the sooner the youngster finds out about it, the better. The old arguments against freedom to portray sexual scenes were that they aroused sexual passions. So what? A photograph of a well-presented meal can arouse the appetite. Children become curious about sex at a very early age. They begin sex play with each other or with themselves almost as soon as they can toddle around. When I was a boy, grown-ups would discourage this. Which stopped the child not at all. If anything, it increased his curiosity. As a rule, he picked up most of his sex education in the streets, discussing the matter with other youngsters no more knowledgeable than he. Do you know that until I was almost fifteen I believed that masturbation would cause your eyes to go weak and your brain to deteriorate, especially if you did it too often? Not that it stopped me for a moment!"

Julian laughed. "I believed the same thing but at that time in my life I imagine I must have averaged about three times a day. My father had some illustrated books that he had picked up in Paris. One day he caught me masturbating while I looked at them and gave me a good walloping."

"Why? Obviously you were learning more about the sex act than you would have talking about it with your schoolmates. Actually, we don't call it pornography very much any more. But the International Data Banks are full of material on sex, fiction and otherwise."

"I guess it makes sense at that," Julian nodded. "Another thing. . . . With a situation as we have today in which ninety-eight percent of the population has full-time leisure, won't the people deteriorate?

Look at the Roman proletariat with its free bread and circuses. The Roman citizen had the equivalent of our Guaranteed Annual Income. And the Empire collapsed.''

Leete nodded agreeably. ''Wasted leisure can be a curse rather than a blessing. Right from the beginning we realized that preparing a student for a job was no longer the basic problem, since so few were needed. So we set our education sights on training our youth for leisure and happiness. Of course, each of us receives training in a field in which we might be chosen to work; but at the same time we also develop ourselves in a half-dozen or more other fields. For instance, since Edith was about ten she's had a strong leaning toward gardening, plants, that sort of thing. It finally wound up with her being chosen on Muster Day to go into agriculture. But she also has a very keen interest in anthropology, archaeology, history, ceramics, and music. Believe me, if she is bounced out of her job, or when she reaches the age of retirement, Edith is going to have no trouble whatsoever in filling her leisure time. Education is the thing.''

Julian said slowly, ''I suppose you're right. Without it, a third of a century ago, a working man often didn't know what to do with his free time. He'd spend a fantastic amount of it watching television, and you can probably remember how bad that was. When I die, I want——''

Dr. Leete choked. ''Die?'' he almost shouted. ''Julian! You . . . you're not contemplating suicide? I know you are unhappy about some of the changes that have taken place and the difficulties you're having acclimating yourself. But suicide isn't the answer.''

"Oh no, you misunderstand. I meant eventually, through natural causes. When I'm older."

Leete shook his head. "You know, during the past few weeks we've had a continual quiz program going on. You ask a hundred questions and by the time we've answered, or half-answered them, we wind up saying *we don't have that any more*. Things like money, banks, cities, pollution, population explosion . . ."

"What's that got to do with my realizing that death——"

"Jule, we don't die any more."

He gaped at the older man.

Leete said hurriedly, "That isn't exactly the way to put it. Of course, everything dies sooner or later. One day the solar system will cool. One day, probably, the galaxy itself will slow down. What I meant was——"

"*What do you mean you don't die any more?*"

"Julian, we keep telling you, human knowledge is doubling every eight years. They defeated cancer shortly after you went into stasis. Heart, kidney, liver diseases are now a thing of the past. So are all contagious diseases. You must realize that medicine is at a point thirty-two times in advance of your period, and even in your time they were making fabulous breakthroughs."

Julian shook his head dumbly. He'd had some wild curves thrown him in the past few weeks, but this one won the game.

Leete said, "Don't you realize that some of the teeth in your head are new? That you've grown new ones? While you were in stasis, we took out all your bridgework, even all your teeth that had been filled, and seeded your jaw. You grew the new teeth while in hibernation."

It simply hadn't occurred to him. All his life he'd had the best of dental care, of course, but he'd had bridges, cavities. He ran his tongue around his mouth. His teeth were now perfect.

The doctor chuckled. "Every few months, after you went into stasis, some great breakthrough would come. Do you know how we conquered venereal disease?"

"No."

"Some genius came up with a new wonder antibiotic. We manufactured a sufficient quantity and then one day, within twenty-four hours, we gave everyone in the country a shot. Everyone—babes in arms, children, adults, the elderly. Nobody escaped: politicians and prostitutes, homosexuals and bishops, the President of the United States and the ambassador from England! The venereal bugs never knew what hit them; they never got the chance to breed up an immune strain. From then on, anybody who entered North America from abroad was given a shot at the border, unless he could prove he'd already had one. Of course, the medicine's formula was immediately divulged to the whole world and similar steps were taken everywhere."

Julian hadn't followed that very well. His brain was in turmoil.

"But . . . immortality . . ."

Leete became slightly impatient. "It's not immortality. As I told you, everything that lives dies sooner or later. The difference is that for a indefinite time you won't die from the old causes. Of course, an accident or suicide will kill you; but otherwise your body cells will continue to replace themselves. You're probably not up on the subject, but scientists have known for a long time that there were some forms of life, mostly very small ones, that never died except by accident. The human animal usually began to slow down in the replacement of its cells in the middle twenties. By the time it reached the sixties, seventies, or eighties, usually some organ would have degenerated to the point where death resulted. To put it simply, science found out what it was that caused the failure to replace body cells.''

''But the population! It must be growing like mad!''

Leete nodded. ''One of our greatest problems. Obviously our birth rate must be kept practically nil. We can afford to bring new children into the world only at the rate the older generations die.''

''But you said they don't die any more.''

''Save through accident or suicide. Suicide, by the way, no longer carries the stigma it once did. Some of our people who attempt to project into the future suspect that the rate will go up considerably as the knowledge explosion continues. The generation gaps will be such that the older generations will find it so difficult to adapt they will no longer wish to continue to live.''

''I know how they feel,'' Julian said. ''But I've seen old people, age seventy or so. If you don't age . . .''

''When the breakthrough came, we were able to so-to-speak freeze each person into the age he had reached. Today, of course, a child ages to adulthood and is given the privilege of deciding the age at which he wishes to remain. Edith chose twenty-five, which I thought very sensible of her.''

Dr. Leete's face was suddenly grim. ''You see, Julian, what we've been telling you about this being no Utopia is quite true. We have our problems. Indeed, heaven only knows how we'll solve some of these that near-immortality has created. We can thank the powers that be, if any, that the desire to have children fell off so drastically just when we needed them so little.''

Chapter Nineteen

The Year 2, New Calendar

It should be borne in mind that there is nothing more difficult to arrange, more doubtful of success, and more dangerous to carry through than initiating changes in a state's constitution. The innovator makes enemies of all those who prospered under the older order . . .
—Niccolo Machiavelli, *The Prince*

EDITH DIDN'T RETURN until late afternoon and by that time Julian was plugging away at his Interlingua. In actuality, by now he had it pretty down pat save for a sufficient vocabulary. The door opened automatically and she entered, a package under one arm.

He looked up from the auto-teacher screen and got to his feet.

"I had to go all the way to the Manhattan Museum." She hesitated before adding, "I still think you are being ridiculous. People don't need guns in this era."

"As you say. However, at least one of the men I am meeting this evening carries one."

He unwrapped the package. "You even managed to get a holster for me!" He took out the gun and checked it. He knew the weapon, an M-35 Browning millimeter. It had a staggered box magazine which could take fourteen cartridges. Some of the Australians in Vietnam had been equipped with them; Julian liked the feel of the gun and had acquired one. He ejected the clip, which he noted to be empty, and threw the breech to be sure there wasn't a round in the barrel.

Edith was eying him apprehensively. "What men are you meeting tonight?"

In the package was a box of cartridges and, sheathed in metal, a combat knife of the type the American marines had carried. Very efficient.

As he fed bullets into the magazine of the Browning, he said to Edith, "The men who think a social change is pending and believe that your father is one of those who are standing in the way. These reform measures he is proposing are concealed measures of reaction—from their viewpoint."

With the heel of his hand he slapped the clip back into the gun, jacked a cartridge into the barrel, and set the safety. Happily, the clothes he was wearing today sported a belt. He attached the holster to it at his left side, under the jacket. He didn't particularly like that kind of a draw, but he was stuck with it unless he wanted to stick the weapon in his belt directly. His clothes didn't provide a pocket big enough for the gun without it being obvious. He strapped on the combat knife in the place his right hip pocket would have occupied if these pants had a hip pocket.

She said, "That's ridiculous. A social change is not pending; it has already taken place. There are still some changes that need to be made and Father is helping further them. But these opponents of his want to go backward, not forward. All change is not progress."

"Meanwhile," he said dryly, "they don't see it that way, and they seem to be on the dedicated side."

"See here, Jule. Admittedly society continues to change, but there are two types: evolution and revolution. Take for example an egg. Inside, it is slowly evolving into a chick, slowly, slowly becoming a more complicated organism. That's evolution. But it is still an egg. It finally grows a beak, little wings, feet, feathers. Evolution. But it is still an egg. Finally, if it is to live, the chick must break the shell and get out. When it does, it is no longer an egg but has become a chick. That's the revolution. The new chick has various problems that haven't all been solved by the revolution of getting out of the eggshell. It has to learn to eat and drink, it has to grow larger, it has to grow more feathers to keep it warm. That's the stage we're at now: learning to grow up. These opponents of Father's are the reactionaries. If they could, they'd probably crawl back into the eggshell."

Julian had to laugh at that. "You'd be surprised how persuasive some of their arguments are," he told her. He went back to his desk and dialed Sean O'Callahan, while Edith stared at him in frustration.

When Sean's face had appeared, Julian asked, "Is there any chance of your little group getting together again this evening?"

"Yes, I would think so. Except for your old friend, Bert Melville, who lives in the Bahamas. Harrison and Ley are living together in a hotel not far from here, and Dave Woolman is currently in residence at the university upgrading his background in radio interferometers." O'Callahan paused. "I would think we could get together within the hour if you had something special in mind."

"I'll be right over," Julian told him, and flicked the phone off.

"What in the world is going on?"

Julian grinned at Edith. "Maybe I'm going over to join up, darling. Possibly I'm one of the chicks that wants to get back into the shell."

He headed for the door.

Somewhat to his surprise, Harrison, Ley, and Woolman were already at Sean O'Callahan's apartment when he arrived. One of the things he wasn't at all clear about was the group's intense interest in him. He had already come to the conclusion that his first meeting with Sean through Edith was a put-up job; the young would-be archaeologist had been sent by the group to contact him.

They all stood at his entrance and Julian went around shaking hands.

He said, naming them in turn, "William Dempsey

Harrison, Fredric Madison Ley, Dave Woolman, Sean O'Callahan. It's a pleasure to see you all again.''

After they were seated once more, and Sean had taken drink orders and delivered them, they looked at Julian expectantly.

He took a sip of his Scotch, a deep breath, and said, ''All right, I'm in. Obviously this world as it is now isn't for me. But the big question in my mind is what you expect of me. I'm thirty years behind the times.''

''We'll tell you all about that,'' Harrison said, obviously pleased with Julian's announcement. ''But first, a little more background. Tell me, after several weeks, what do you think of Academician Leete?''

Julian grunted and shrugged. ''Kind of a fuddy-duddy and in full agreement with the way society is run today.''

''He sure as hell is,'' Sean said. ''If he had his way, we'd get to the point where 99.9 percent of the population had nothing to do and everybody would be sitting around on their asses painting or writing poetry.''

Harrison made a rather abrupt gesture at Sean, silencing him. He said to Julian, ''I have a confession to make. I am not a resident of this area, Julian West.''

Julian fixed his eyes on him, waiting.

Harrison said, ''Mr. West, we need a man of charisma. We need a leader. My residence is actually in Seattle, where I am one of the three Presidors of the Society for Return to Civilization. The Society sent me here to contact you.''

"I am sure you don't need someone thirty years behind the times."

Woolman bent forward; his voice was sincere. "That is exactly what we need. A man who knew the world when it was a world of action, full of life, aggression, ambition. A man who stops at nothing to achieve his ends. A leader of the old school."

Harrison said, "You probably have little idea of the reaction among the United American people to your reawakening. You have been kept shielded from them by Leete while going through this period of acclimation. But the people as a whole are fascinated by you and the romance of your story. Given the spark that we need to mobilize them behind us, you would be ideal to step into the leadership position."

"How many of us are there now in this Society for Return to Civilization?"

"Several tens of thousands."

"That's not very many for a country as large as United America."

"We told you the other night of the potential following, given a spark to unite them."

Julian took another small sip and another deep breath and said, "All right, we've come to the nitty-gritty. What spark?"

Harrison looked around at the others. One by one they nodded.

His eyes came back to Julian. "This is a very well-kept secret, unknown even to the membership of the organization save for the other two Presidors of the Society, we here in this room, and several on Luna. It will continue to remain a secret even after having been put into operation."

Julian nodded.

Harrison said very slowly, ''As we told you, Dave Woolman here is head of the Radio Astronomy Observatory on Luna. He has infiltrated his staff with our followers. Currently his radio interferometers are trained on——''

''Just a minute. What's a radio interferometer?'' Julian asked.

Woolman took over. ''Essentially a radio telescope with a bank of antennas, rather than just one.''

''Go on.''

Harrison took a slug of his own drink. ''He is to return to the moon tomorrow, and shortly after he will begin receiving the first radio signals from intelligent life forms from another star, another planetary system.''

Julian stared at him. ''And . . .''

''The signals will be understandable . . . and hostile. This other life form is aggressive to the point of paranoia. They cannot accept the idea of another intelligent life form. They have been receiving our radio signals for some years and hence have been able to decipher our language, so it is possible for them to communicate with us. For the past ten years, they have been building a military space fleet. They are on the way to attack.''

''Jesus!'' Julian exclaimed.

''They aim to destroy the whole world.''

Julian looked from Harrison to Woolman. ''The plan is to fake it, obviously. But aren't there other radio telescopes that could check up on you, refute your claims?''

Woolman shook his head. ''We're the only one on

Luna. The others don't have a fraction of our power and freedom from interference."

Julian went back to Harrison. "And then?"

"And then our organization begins an all-out clamor for a revived military machine. Uniting the country to mobilize for defense. The appointment of a strong man to lead us. We expect that overnight millions will flock to our banner. After a few days, according to how things go, how fast the avalanche develops, we will set up a cry for you to be appointed supreme head of the mobilization."

Julian said negatively, "There are thousands of men still alive who held down higher ranks than I did and who saw at least as much combat as I did."

"They are in their sixties, seventies, or even older. However, many of them are already members of the Society. You will appoint them as your deputies, your assistants. There are other organization members ready to step into your ranks."

"Then what happens?"

"At first we will basically retain the present socioeconomic system. As we become stronger and dominate the economy and the government, we will begin to whittle away at it in the name of defense against the alien attackers. To a great extent we will have to play it by ear. But when we are through, we will hold the country in an iron grip."

"I suppose we would be for an eventual world government?"

Harrison shook his head. "Certainly not. That is one of Leete and his group's least desirable goals. Man makes his greatest progress under the stimulation of international disagreements, including war.

Just look at World War Two. Under its pressure were developed such things as nuclear fission, jet aircraft, the German V2, the first spacecraft. Besides, having rival nations puts you in a position to control the people. If they become restive, you stir up a bit of trouble abroad and unite them behind you. It's an old Roman adage.''

Julian snorted. ''So you're all ready to go, and I'm to be your man of charisma.'' He paused. ''It's the most harebrained scheme I've ever heard and it won't work.''

Sean O'Callahan flushed in surprised anger. ''It'll work whether or not you come in, West. You're not indispensable to the plan.''

''No, but I sure as hell can throw a monkeywrench into it.'' Julian brought out his transceiver from his pocket. It was open for transmission and had been since he had entered the apartment.

He said, ''Observe the latest in electronic bugs, although that's not what they had in mind when it was invented. This thing has been set to record everything that has been said in this room in the International Data Banks. When we put it into the news tomorrow, Academician Leete and I, the whole world will have a good laugh at your scheme to bollix up the observatory and claim messages from the phony alien intelligent life.''

Harrison snapped, ''Fredric!''

Fredric Ley was seated directly across from Julian about twenty feet away. His right hand had already disappeared beneath his coat during the last few minutes of conversation. Now he brought out a revolver and directed it at Julian.

Julian contemplated him for a moment before unbuttoning his jacket so that the others could see that he, too, bore a gun.

He said conversationally to Ley, "I had already figured you for Harrison's bodyguard. You said that you were in Vietnam . . ."

Ley rapped out, "Sean. Go get his gun."

Julian shifted his gaze to Sean O'Callahan, who definitely looked uncomfortable. Julian said, "Don't move, Sean, or you're a dead man. God forgive me, I have enough dead men on my hands."

Ley rasped, "I've got you covered, wise guy. We have some of our people in the data banks; we can have that tape wiped. And we've got you and can find a place to hold you for as long as necessary."

Julian sighed and said, "If you *were* in 'Nam you probably stocked PX shelves. For one thing, that revolver you're carrying is a thirty-two-caliber Colt. No combat man would ever carry one. I've been hit various times by more gun than that. Besides, I suspect you're a lousy shot. I'm betting I can get this gun out and finish you before you can finish me, Ley. So any time you want to start shooting, go ahead."

Dave Woolman said in horror, "You're mad!"

Harrison ordered, "Take him, Fredric."

Julian grinned confidently, seemingly completely at ease.

There were blisters of cold sweat on the bodyguard's forehead and his face was pale. His gun hand trembled slightly.

Julian said conversationally, "You're yellow, Ley. Either start shooting or drop that gun. I'm going to count to five. One . . . two . . . three . . ."

The pistol dropped with a thud to the carpet. Fredric Ley's face was slack with fear.

Julian said pleasantly, "Any of you boys want to pick it up?"

Harrison alone even looked at the weapon.

Julian stood up and looked around at each of them in turn.

Finally, he let his eyes rest on their leader. He said, "I looked up some of those people of charisma, the great leaders that you said the computers would never have chosen for their Aptitude Quotient. Catherine the Great was only great in bed; she was a slob. Hitler was insane, and proved it; you're right that the computers wouldn't have chosen him—and shouldn't have. Alexander the Great conquered Persia because his father, Philip, who *would* have been chosen by the computers, had built up an army that was the best and most experienced in the world; his son Alexander was a drunk. Grant was a second-rate general and a worse president. The North should have won that war in half the time considering their economy and larger population. Lee kept the fighting going a couple of years after it shouldn't have been possible any longer. Lee, by the way, graduated top man in his West Point class and undoubtedly would have been chosen by the computers. Lincoln and Edison were both geniuses and self-educated. As Leete mentioned, they would have surfaced in any society."

Suddenly he was tired. "The hell with it," he said. "I'll take the computer's choices any day compared to you characters."

He turned and left, knowing very well that none of them would go for the gun when his back was turned.

Aftermath

The mechanical educator could impress on the brain in a matter of a few minutes, knowledge and skills which might otherwise take a lifetime to acquire . . . Impressing information directly onto the brain, so that we can know things without ever learning them, seems . . . impossible today . . . Yet the mechanical educator—or some technique which performs similar functions—is such an urgent need that civilization cannot continue for many more decades without it. The knowledge of the world is doubling every ten years—and the rate is itself increasing. Already, twenty years of schooling are insufficient; soon we will have died of old age before we have learned to live, and our entire culture will have collapsed owing to its incomprehensible complexity.

—Arthur C. Clarke

IT WAS TWO WEEKS following the Society for Return to Civilization farce. The organization had dissolved before the laughter of the country as a whole when Julian's taped conversation was played on the news. It was broadcast in its entirety, from the moment he had entered Sean O'Callahan's apartment and one by one shook hands with each of the room's occupants, to the point where he had finally turned his back on them contemptuously and left.

The three Leetes were seated with Julian in their living room.

Dr. Leete looked from Julian to Edith and back again. He said, "You two are in love, aren't you?"

Martha looked up from her embroidery in mild surprise.

Edith said impatiently, "Don't be ridiculous, Father. You know very well that a permanent relationship between Jule and me isn't practical considering our different backgrounds. The gulf is too great."

"You didn't answer my question," Raymond Leete pressed. "The institution of romantic love isn't as dead as all that. When I was Julian's age I fell quite madly in love with your mother." He smiled over at his wife, who smiled back but kept her peace. "And frankly, I still feel the same way. I don't think that one generation is going to completely wipe the feeling away, despite all the changes that have taken place in the relationship between the sexes."

He turned to Julian. "About six months ago, some colleagues of mine specializing in the human brain came up with a breakthrough. I'll try and keep the terminology to that which you will be able to understand. It involves the transfer of accumulated knowledge from one person's brain to another's."

Even Edith looked at him blankly. "I haven't heard of it," she said. "No mention has been made in the scientific news."

"It hasn't been tested."

Julian asked, his voice trembling slightly, "Why not?"

"They're afraid to test it on a human being."

Martha asked, "It has been tested on animals?"

"Yes. First on rats. We took two sets of rats and trained them in different ways, using several sets for controls, and then put them in the device. It worked. That is, we were able to transfer the training of one to the mind of the other. The rat who acquired the knowledge immediately knew everything that his partner had ever learned."

Julian phrased his question carefully: "Why are they afraid to try it on a human being?"

"Two days later, the rats who received the information artificially all went insane. The rats who had provided the information transferred were quite all right, and still retained the material themselves."

Edith said, "So the experiments were discontinued?"

"No. They tried it next on rabbits with the same result: insanity ensued."

Julian took a deep breath. "And then?"

"They tried it on a more complex life form, the dog. Once again, the transfer was successful, but the dogs involved went mad."

It was Edith's turn to say, "And then, Father?"

He looked at her. "They tried it on a chimpanzee, and once again it worked. But on this occasion the animal retained both its new artifically acquired information and its sanity."

"And that is where the experiment is to date?" Martha asked.

"No. They next used two orangutans. Only two because that was all they could locate of the rather scarce anthropoid apes, which many authorities consider the most intelligent of the primates short of man himself."

Edith said, "And it worked again?"

"Yes. To this date, at least, neither the several chimps nor the one orangutan have shown any signs of distress and they have all continued to retain their artificially induced knowledge."

Julian said, his voice low, "Why are you afraid to try it on a man?"

Leete sighed. "Isn't it obvious? Man's brain is the most complicated organism which we know of in the universe. It is an extremely delicate organ. The scientists involved do not want to risk the sanity of a human volunteer. On the other hand, they can't forward the experiment without such a volunteer."

Julian said, "You mean that if Edith and I were put in this device, all of the accumulated knowledge in her brain would be transferred to mine—without her being affected in any manner?"

"Yes—if it works on human beings."

Julian looked at Edith. "What are we waiting for, darling?"

Mack Reynolds

FRITZ LEIBER

06218	**The Big Time** $1.25
30301	**Green Millennium** $1.25
53330	**Mindspider** $1.50
76110	**Ships to the Stars** $1.50
79152	**Swords Against Death** $1.25
79173	**Swords and Deviltry** $1.50
79162	**Swords Against Wizardry** $1.25
79182	**Swords in the Mist** $1.25
79222	**The Swords of Lankhmar** $1.25
95146	**You're All Alone** 95¢

Available wherever paperbacks are sold or use this coupon.

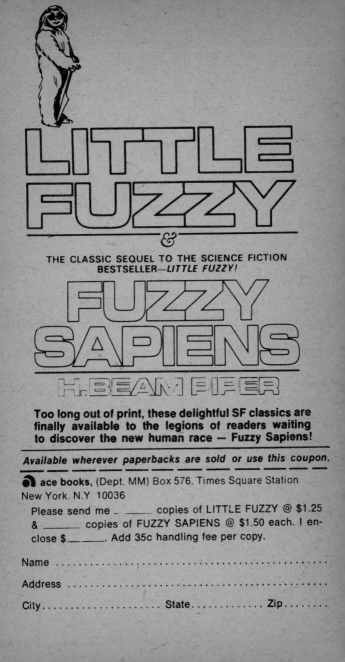